A Thousand Thugs

SPECIAL EDITION FOR PRISONERS

a novel by
DARRYL E. BUCHANNAN

DARRYL E. BUCHANNAN

A Thousand Thugs
SPECIAL EDITION FOR PRISONERS

Text © 2017 Darryl E. Buchannan
www.FAB-Fresh-Air-Books.com

Cover Design: Ishan Birchett
I.B. Graphics, Worcester, MA
Original Logo Design: Mark Thomas

Interior Text Design /Art Direction: Lisa Breslow Thompson
LisaThompsonGraphicDesign.com

All rights reserved. No part of this book may be used or reproduced by any means, graphic, electronic or mechanical, including photocopying, recording or taping, or by any information storage retrieval systems without the express written permission of the publisher, author and/or illustrator.

Unless otherwise noted, all illustrations, photographs, etc. are courtesy of the author.

Library of Congress Control Number: 2017915779
ISBN: 9781941573174

Published by
Fresh Air Books
PO Box 511
Hudson, MA 01749

In conjunction with
Damianos Publishing
1630 Concord Street
Framingham, MA 01701 USA
www.DamianosPublishing.com

Produced through Silver Street Media by Bridgeport National Bindery
Agawam, MA USA
First printed 2017

CONTENTS

Message from the Author iv

Acknowledgements and Shout Outs..vii

A THOUSAND THUGS PART ONE

Chapters 1 – 18 1-100

A THOUSAND THUGS PART TWO

Chapters 19 – 30 101-132

Epilogue – "Gangsta No More"..134

A Thousand Thugs – **PRISONERS EDUCATIONAL COMPONENT**..........................143

DARRYL E. BUCHANNAN

A THOUSAND THUGS – MESSAGE FROM THE AUTHOR

First and foremost madd love and appreciation to everyone who supported this effort and copped my book. Especially those in my hood and city who patiently waited for this book to drop, and rode all the bumps, pauses and restarts with me, as I battled and struggled against my own personal demons (addiction) to keep this dream of writing books and launching my very own Publishing Company "Fresh Air Books" alive. It's been a tough assignment, but I got it done! I know that the language used to communicate this story will rub some the wrong way. Words such as bitch, nigga etc. which is the language of the youth culture and could be found regularly in rap videos, music, as well as movies can make some uncomfortable and I understand. Initially I thought about not writing this story, and just parking the idea in the trash can of my memories because I felt that there was no way to keep the authenticity of the characters without using their language. After further contemplation and soul searching, asking myself how important it was to tell this story, I had to question why I was writing this story. I mean was it for my own self-gratification or possibly to save a young person from traveling down the same destructive path I traveled? I reached the conclusion, and felt their stories were much more important to tell than not tell. I also decided there was no point in telling their story if I couldn't be 100% honest and true to form. So in the end the language is intentional, as I felt an obligation to stay true to the times, culture and its language in order to reach those that I am trying to reach through my book.

A Thousand Thugs is NOT a glorification of violence, gangs or drugs, but instead an interpretation of the world I grew up in and see when I go outside or look out my window. The language is what I hear falling from young people's mouths, and also some grown-ups' mouths as I ride the subway or buses. So what may appear as a bunch of curse words on paper, may be the story of some kid's life, who is living in a world where it's killed or be killed. A world where most do not expect to live past the age of twenty. My mission in writing this story is to provoke thought, and to have a young person who may be out there toting guns, gangbanging and living this negative deathstyle to think and rethink about the consequences and also possibilities.

This book is not mine, it's Ours, and belongs to all the homies who walked the same streets I walked. Hustled on the same blocks I hustled on, and hit up the same bodegas I hit up. Many times I wanted to give up and just park this pen. But each time the thought of quitting put a full court press on me, I could hear my Beautiful Mother's voice telling me to "Pick up that pen, boy." I would also remember and think about the lil homies in my hood who like me have dreams that they don't believe, or have reason to believe, could come true, because they are being spoon fed deception and bombarded with crippling messages by a society that tells them they are nothing and never will be anything.

Unfortunately as they look around their environment, they find confirmation that supports this destructive lie. Yeah, I write for those growing up inside concrete jungles, who are surrounded by negative, empty and dreamless influences, where their role models are drug dealers, junkies, criminals and gangbangers, those who are most likely to have a parent or family member, caught up in the grips of addiction or sitting behind prison walls, roaming around hopelessly and the only message they receive about escaping the chaos, poverty and negativity that envelopes them is like B.I.G. said, "either sling crack rocks or have a wicked jump shot."

DARRYL E. BUCHANNAN

Thinking about the lil homies in my hood and all across the world kept me pushing this pen. I wanted to show them that no matter what your circumstances or where you come from, you can still overcome the odds and make your dreams come true. And in some ways I am proof of that. In my own life I've been through more stuff than a fly swimming in doo-doo and on more than one occasion so close to hell that you can smell the smoke on my clothes. But if completing this book could pass a message of hope to a lil homey with nothing but a pocketful of dreams, and get him to believe and dream outside the negativity and failure that surrounds him, then me not giving up, and making this happen was well worth the struggle.

Not to mention I wanted to put a great Kool Aid type of smile on a Very Beautiful Woman's face, who has been my biggest cheerleader all of my life, and is now sitting up in Heaven looking down and rooting for me. **MOM, I LOVE YOU, WE DID IT!**

Darryl Buchannan
Author of *A Thousand Thugs*

ACKNOWLEDGEMENTS AND SHOUT OUTS

Extra love to the one true God, Jesus Christ, who placed this creative energy inside of a little boy from the Bishop Markham Housing Project, and knew that one day, the world would take notice. All Praise is His not mines.

To my Mom, who happens to be the most beautiful woman who ever walked this earth. It is her undying love, support, and belief in me and my abilities that kept me spilling ink across blank pages. It is her spirit that never ever allowed me to give up, even in the most darkest of times. I love you with every ounce and fiber of my being. It is because of you that my stories will be shared with the world. When the whole world said I couldn't it was your voice that said I could. Thank you for believing. I miss you, and if my tears could build a staircase, I'd climb up to heaven, and bring you back done here with me. My deepest wish was that you could be here to see this work, but then again you are here in spirit. Again, thank you for putting up with a knucklehead like me. You're the best.

A special shout to my two heartbeats, Ty and Jayden. I know it hasn't been easy for all of us, but you two put up with a lot of my B.S. I hope that in some way, this book will show you I'm still fighting to leave you something. Love is love. We are one.

Ms. Carolyn Ruf, my truest friend in all the world. You have been there when this whole thing was in its embryo stage. You believed when no one else could or would. You stuck by me, when my world was collapsing all around me. Found me, when I was lost in my own destruction. You have been my voice of reason when the madness outweighed the logic.

Thank you for all your sacrificing, all your patience with me. You never stopped believing. You saw this vision when no one else did. We both knew we could get it done. I must admit without you, it possibly would have been a dream that died inside of me. I'm indebted to you. Hope all our stories and Fresh Air Books will conquer the world.

Special Shout Out To My Family, the Buchannans: Melinda, Judith, Vernon, Ameatrice, Terence, Maria, and ... the whole Buchannan Tree, nieces, nephews, cousins, aunts, uncles. Without all of you there would be no me. Love you all. Believe in your dreams. This is YOUR BOOK. I'm nothing without you all. Love every one of you. Especially To My Big Brother Vernon "Popie" Buchannan. Love ya 1000 times extra.

To all those who believed and rode with me from Day One! Peter Delgado, Trisha Delgado, Stephanie Clement, Tommy Bowers, Dion, Masada and Diamond Jones, George "Spider" Dudley, Charlie Banks.

My Mentors: Mr. Lennie Spitale, Bud Woods, Pastor Jim Morrison, Pastor Doug Wambolt, the whole Greater Grace family, especially Pastor Renaldo Brown, who's doing God's work in Africa. You go, brother.

Richetta Woods and family, love you guys. You always stood by me and never passed judgement. You were always encouraging me, and standing in my corner. Thanks for all the love Big Sis.

Mr. James Mitchell, my Bro, you always stood by me no matter what and never passed judgement. A man is lucky if in life he has friends. I only got a few "true friends'. You are definitely one of them.

Tony "Andy" Pires, one of my biggest motivators, who kept pushing me to write. You believed and always, always no matter how low I fell, you would come offering a hand up. I count you as a true friend.

A THOUSAND THUGS

SPECIAL THANKS TO:

Katy Cody, like a phoenix arises from its ashes, our love has been beaten, battered, broken. All of the storms have tried us, and no matter what, we have managed to stick together, and overcome the madness. Hope my presence helps you to become a better you, for your presence has helped me became a better me. Appreciate you much!

To The Bridge House for giving me a safe, positive, and constructive environment to refocus, rethink, and rebuild a more productive life.

Recovery Connection, Marlborough, MA: For seven years you all have been like family to me. You've stood by me, always with a smile, love and acceptance. I got nothing but love for all of you. And a heart full of appreciation - Angela, Kelly, Brandon and the whole Recovery Connection Family. "Together We Can."

Roland's House: When the storms of life came, you always were there to help shelter me from the storms, and put me aback on my feet - Gwen, Kenny, Mike, and Elizabeth.

Middlesex Sheriff's Department: Thanks for the encouragement, assistance and help in putting the pieces back together You are definitely appreciated – Deputy Leah Lewis, Louie Diaz, Martha Newsham.

To all those locked behind the walls, keep dreaming, never give up.

Special thanks to my Publisher, Ms. Lynne Damianos and Graphic Designer, Lisa Thompson.

DARRYL E. BUCHANNAN

Salvatore Castiello

Remembering Sal. One of the first to show my book love. He was one hell of a dude. R.I.P. Bro.

"Shout out to my big bro Darryl Buchannan for writing this book A Thousand Thugs. It really hits home for me. It's a powerful story of being torn between the streets and glory and the struggle of perseverance through adversity ... and just like Faze says "The game should be sold and not told." If you wanna know the story, go cop you a copy when it drops!!!"

Sal Castiello on September 28, 2017

"There have been many hood novels, but this is ... 'one of the best'. By providing personal insight into gang life, the author keeps you turning the pages. 'A must read.' ~*Mark Thomas, Roxbury*

Mark is currently at Norfolk and has served more than 38 years of a life sentence at MCI institutions. His Fresh Air Books logo design and original B.A.B.N.A.B. T shirt designs are his way of reaching over the wall. He is a free man inside.

A THOUSAND THUGS

A portion of the proceeds from this book will go the fights against cancer and addiction in the name of

Mrs. Louella R. Buchannan

To all those locked behind the walls keep dreaming, never give up. Shout Out to All My Mill City Peeps and Homeys!

---

*This book and anything and everything I do that is positive,
I do always in the strength of my homey
George Avont Tyree
Never ever forgotten.
Love you Bro*

Today Darryl, who has spent 28 years incarcerated, has found a way out and a way to stay out. He is a published author and founder of this publishing company, F.A.B. and also B.A.B.N.A.B., an Anti-Bullying/Violence/Gang Initiative. Darryl accepts invitations to speak on the topics of drug addiction and incarceration, the two things that consumed many years of his life, and recovery. His goal is to give hope and dispel the myth of the gangsta/thug lifestyle.

PART ONE

CHAPTER ONE

"YO, WE GOT NEXT!" yelled a tall and skinny light skinned kid with a crazy ass pep in his step, walking towards the handball court with his boy on his heels. He was the exact opposite of his homey, and was madd midget type: short and chubby. The bugged out thing was he looked almost fat, and he seemed to be wobbling as if one of his legs was shorter than the other. It made him move off balance like he was about to fall over. (Not to mention he was crazy black and could have been mistaken for the color blue.) They both had the numbers 617 tatted on their throats, and the words Beantown on their hands in the same exact place. They pushed up on the court as if they had all the swag in the world.

"And you know we gonna whip that ass," the short one said confidently.

"Man, you niggas is straight bums," answered a kid with rough looking unkempt single braids in his hair. They looked like nappy dreads that was clocking the game and shagging balls.

"That's a fact. Besides, me and my boy got next, so just fall back and watch how real niggas from Mill City get it rocking. Shit, all we do is trap and fuck with this blue ball in our hood," he said seriously. That caused niggas who were watching to say "Oooohh!", trying to amp shit up.

"Yo, you sound madd dumb right now", the skinny kid said. "When it's our ups if you niggas are wit' it and still on the court, we can put some canteen on it."

"Man, you ain't said nothing but a word. Say less, we can definitely put some bread on it, facts," said the kid with the funny braids.

"Ya'll little city niggas from Lowell think ya'll good at everything. You don't know jack about how Beantown niggas get down."

"Yo, you can press the e-brake on your mouth about Lowell," the kid said seriously fucking with his braids.

"Whatever G. You got that. But on some real shit just be on the court when I get there, cause it's on, and popping," skinny kid said smiling and giving his boy daps.

"You already know what's up" he answered with a fucked up look on his face and peeling off his prison jumpsuit.

It was crazy hot in the concrete closure as about forty teens, mostly black and Latino, filled the cage. They were dressed in orange jumpsuits with DYS (Department of Youth Services) stamped across the front in bold letters. It could have passed for a giant holding tank, except there was a basketball rim mounted onto the south wall, and pull up and dip bars along the north wall. Prisoners used these to work out, and release some of the stress of being locked up. Dangerous and ugly rows of razor wire outlining the top perimeter of the cage were put there to let them know there was nothing happening on the escape tip.

Some of the prisoners, mostly Latinos and members of the Latin Kings Gang, were deeply caught up watching their brothers play a game of two on two on the handball court.

The handball court was their spot, and they held it down. The blacks held down the basketball court, which only consisted of one hoop. So there was no full court jumping off.

The whites, who were definitely outnumbered, basically just got in where they fit in. They did have a little clique called CWB (Crazy White Boys). They weren't straight suckers, but getting a win on some beef type shit was slim or none. So they just stayed on the low profile and did their bid quietly.

Other prisoners, representing different gangs and hoods from throughout Massachusetts, were posted up with a thug's posture with their backs against the concrete wall. They were clocking every movement in the cage with menacing glares and ice grills on their young faces. The move was to look as tough and hardcore as possible to ward off anyone who would perceive them as soft or weak. When you're in a jungle like this, it is better to look like a predator rather than prey. If anyone peeped any weakness in you, you would most definitely be considered food for the whole cellblock with niggas putting the smash on you, and checking you for your canteen and shit. So everybody fronted, and had their chests puffed up, even the sucker niggers.

In the far corner of the cage was a circle of prisoners bobbing their heads, listening to a couple of kats battle rap over the blazing sound of a nigga who was getting it in and beat boxing Dougie Fresh style.

Roslindale lock up was located on the outskirts of Boston. It was the state's Juvenile Maximum Security Prison, and over the years had developed a rep for being a Gladiators School for Offenders who were high risk. Inmates were high risk security threats, or just straight thugged the fuck out, and didn't give two fucks about shit on the bricks, with a kill-a-nigga-quick type mentality.

Madd heads were there for some of the craziest crimes, ranging anywhere from dangerous assaults, rape, gang violence and gang affiliation to murder in the first degree. Many were locked down in Roslindale because they were on some straight knucklehead shit, and causing ruckus in less secure facilities. They were transferred there to give them an attitude adjustment, and tune them into the rules, hoping to put a full court press on their behavior.

The prison was buck wild at times, full of super-predators and dangerous, heartless youths who always had some type of situation and beef going on. Not only was it crazy overcrowded, packing niggas in the blocks like sardines, but it was filled to the brim. It was also filled to the brim with teens who were straight gang members reppin' different sets or color. They were already beefing and killing each other on the bricks, so it was definitely popping off onsite, all day every day. The violence got crazy turnt up especially whenever an enemy came through.

The administration had a tough time keeping the violence on lock. They did the best they could to minimize and put a speed bump in the drama by gathering intel, closely monitoring those affiliated, and stamping their file with STG (Security Threat Group) as soon as they came through the gates.

They isolated the shot callers and hardcore bangers from the general population and from those they knew were not bout it, and were faking the funk only pledging their allegiance to a gang and getting down just for a title or protection.

The real cold hearted hotheads was locked down twenty-three hours a day in their cells on the dolo, where they had to use that hour to make phone calls, take showers and catch rec. There was never enough time to do all three, so most prisoners went without showering, choosing instead to holla at their peeps on the phone, bust out a few pull-ups and just take a bird bath in their sink in the cell.

Every day during recreation period the prisoners would hold a cipher where they would battle rap each other and put their rhyming skills on front street to see who had the dopest and tightest flow. The winner of the battle got bragging rights and the green light to scream out and big up his hood on the cellblock, not to mention win whatever was bet between those battling. Shit, some niggas walked away fucked up, losing their Reeboks, canteen and Walkmans. Those that fronted and assed bet and lost were sent straight to PC (Protective Custody) to live with the rats and rapists who were the bitch niggas that got no love in the joint. Every real ass nigga hated and would smash them on site.

When Harlem Valentine got to Roslindale he caught wind of the cipher. A kat named MoneyTwice from Dorchester had been the facility's rap god. He had been holding down the crown for an ill minute with a tight kung fu type grip after knocking off a kat named Crispy from Lawrence who was top dawg when he got there.

Harlem was madd amped, and couldn't wait to get on the rec deck, and get fresh on MoneyTwice's heels. In Harlem's mind he knew his skills were fire, and the crown should belong to the Mill City, his hood. He had every intention of going after it, and putting on for his city.

On the day of their battle, none of the prisoners worked out or played ball. There was so much hype through the week about this kat Harlem being the shit that anticipation on the cellblock was heavy. It was looked forward to like niggas on the street anticipating the Mayweather and Pacquiao fight. Even the COs were looking forward to it because they were hoping the competition would give birth to niggas going at it on the physical tip. That gave them a chance to run down on niggas with their NBC (nigger be cool) sticks.

Harlem was knee deep into spitting flames and putting the lyrical smash on MoneyTwice when his homey Fly, who had just come back from Lowell Superior Court, pushed up on the cipher. He pulled Harlem to the side on some emergency shit, and told him about the scram Joker from the South Side that had rolled up on their block. He shot it up on some reckless sucker shit, hitting up their big homey Lick's mom and lil sis as they were leaving Brothers Pizza. Fly pulled Harlem's coat to the fact that he was in court with the clown ass nigga who was now downstairs in booking being processed and about to pull show on their cellblock.

"Say word?" Harlem said all hyped up.

"Yo, for real, for real my nigga. That nigga is in the building," Fly answered.

"That's what's up. That bitch ass nigga is mine, dawg. I'm going at him dolo, ya heard? And if there is anything left of him when I get done, it's yours," Harlem said looking Fly straight in his eyes.

"That's a fact, yo. But that nigga don't deserve no fair one, but it's your call, my nigga. If that's how you want to play it, then it is what it is. But yo, make sure you save some for me. Aiigh't?" Fly said reluctantly.

"That's a bet. You got that my nigga," Harlem answered with a look on his face that seemed like he was smiling and frowning at the same time.

By the look on Fly's face you could tell he was kind of tight about not being able to put in work on the sucka nigga. He felt that the nigga didn't deserve no type of mercy, and that all the Fives on the block should rush his cell. But Harlem was the Leader of his crew the North Common Fives, so whatever he said was bond, and he had to roll with it. No doubt he felt some type of way, but kept it to himself. After all he wanted a piece of Joker also because Lick was also his big homey, and he wanted to get some get back and represent for his peeps.

You could see the anger on Harlem's grill and the vein popping out on the sides of his face screamed that his temperature was percolating and risen straight to the top. Harlem had planned to serve him up something proper and beat him as close to death as he could without killing him. For he knew that Joker's last breath belonged and was already claimed by his big homey.

Lick was already on deck waiting for the sucker nigga to pull show up MCI Shirley Max. There was no question that Lick was going to body him for what he did to his fam. Lick was an OG, and straight gangster with his murder game. He had put in madd work on the streets of Lowell, and you couldn't mention his name without mentioning murder in the same sentence. He was already serving three life without parole sentences for going on a murder spree killing three rivals from the Belvidere section, so he had nothing to lose. Murdering Joker was just something light. Truth be told, it was nothing but rec to a nigga like Lick. Shit, what the courts going to do, give him another life sentence? They already took his life and he only had one. So killing Joker was nothing but a free meal, and you could bet your bottom dollar the big homey was going to eat.

Harlem walked back to the cipher where everyone was waiting totally amped and turnt up with his adrenaline racing through his body a hundred miles an hour. He opened his mouth and let loose and finished spittin' the illest lyrics from right where he left off, putting the finishing touches on MoneyTwice's ass.

Mill City is the illest City
Where they shoot to kill you-City
Big face bills-City
Turn ugly to pretty-City
Shitty to gritty-City
We fresh and stay litty-City
Shorts, nah we don't take any-City

When he finished spraying venom, the prisoners went dumb stupid, hugging and giving him crazy daps letting him know his shit had their ears stuck like glue! There was no question to anyone there that he had just snatched the crown off of MoneyTwice's head. And by the look on MoneyTwice's grill you could tell he knew his time of being the man was up, and that his best bet was to go back to the lab and tighten his game up. Because the nigga from Lowell had just came at him spitting fire out of his mouth like a dragon. Not one to hate, MoneyTwice kept it a buck and gave Harlem daps and his props on some real dawg shit.

While the niggas was all caught up in the hype of what just happened the loudspeaker came on interrupting the celebration ordering prisoners back to their cells. Niggas made sure they didn't miss their doors, cause that shit would cost them seventy-two hours straight locked down.

"Yo, Harlem," yelled a familiar and raspy voice.

Harlem turned around in the middle of the tier after grabbing his shower bag off the fence and saw MoneyTwice.

"What's popping?" Harlem answered with a kool aid smile on his face.

"Yo, bout time a nigga came through here with a tongue on fire, but on some real shit, hold that win loosely cause I'm comin' back with my Capitol A game my nigga," he said with a serious grin.

"Bring it," Harlem said. "You better come correct dude, cause truth be told that was only something light."

Harlem lifted his arms in the air and with his fingers formed the letters MC.

"That's right Mill City is in the motherfucking hizzouse. And for those that didn't get the memo and think they got something for me, you already know how I'm doing it. I'm gonna rep Lowell until I bounce up out of this piece and that's on dead dawgs," he said, and turned and walked down the tier toward his cell like a pimp who just got thousands from his hoe. ❏

CHAPTER TWO

HARLEM WAS IN HIS CELL taking the flicks of his girl Lauren and his homeys off his cell wall, and packing up his little bit of property. He had already hit his homey Fly and the rest of the Lowell niggas off with the canteen and shit they made from running the block store, where they charged two for one on snacks, food and cosmetics. He knew he was on his way to the box and would probably be locked down on ice for an ill minute, after he beat the breaks off the scram nigga Joker.

It would be his second major ticket for violence. He caught the first ticket at Lowell District Court when he got held on $100,000 bail. He called the Judge and everybody in that motherfucker nothing but racist bitches and then spit on his lawyer, who he felt cold sold him out with a half ass pitch for a bail argument. The lawyer had come off like Johnny Cochran when he came down to see Harlem in the holding tank, where he was waiting to go in front of the judge. Shit, Harlem thought for sure he would get him a bail he could handle. But when dude got in front of the Judge his mouth was empty of a real defense. Harlem was tight and spit on him and started going after him. The lawyer bitched up and yelled for help. The court officers rushed Harlem and brought him downstairs to the court lock up. They tried to literally drag him and rough him up, so he began beefing with them.

When the Middlesex Sheriffs came to pick him up, the court officers told them about him wildin' in the courtroom, and what went down and to give Harlem the knuckleheads treatment when he got back to Roslindale for acting up in the courtroom.

When he got back to Roslindale they immediately threw him in isolation, and charged him with four counts of assault and battery on the Court Officers and his lawyer and contempt of court.

While in isolation the Superintendent, who was a cold blooded asshole, personally came to the hole to see him. And he told Harlem he would be spending ninety days in there, and then after that if he decided to let him out, he had better be on his best behavior, and that if he started any trouble or come up on the tiers with his 'don't give a fuck' attitude, he would make sure Harlem regretted his stay at Roslindale.

Now packing his shit for his trip to the box, he dismissed the thought of consequences and what the Superintendent threatened him with, and couldn't wait to see Joker and put his hands and foot to his ass. All niggas from the Mill knew what it was when they came at his hood. It was ghetto news that the North Common was not to be fucked with, and this off brand motherfucker had violated his block in a major way and he had been waiting for him to show up for a minute now.

Harlem had read in the Lowell Sun a few weeks before about Joker being captured out in New York, where he had been hiding, and that he was in the process of being extradited back to Mass to face the stunt he pulled. Now that day had come full circle, and it was time to let the lame know what it was with the North Side. Because nobody ever came through their hood causing ruckus and got away with it. Nobody. Not even the devil himself could.

Harlem remembered those words coming from a big homey who schooled him when he was just knee high to a squirrel sitting on top of the roof as a look-out for the niggas. The older heads made sure the lil homeys got the game raw, and kept it pure, so that anyone who came through their hood trippin' on some bullshit, knew it was nothing but smoke on site, and all beefs with the North Side lasted a lifetime.

When Joker pulled show on the block Harlem peeped him at the COs station receiving his cell assignment, and then watched what cell he was going to. You could tell the nigga was crazy nervous, and he looked madd shook. As soon as Joker walked into his cell Harlem ran in his cell and was on him before he even got the chance to make his bed.

It happened so quick that God didn't get the news before he stole on him, and began raining blows on him. All Joker could do was cover up like a bitch to try to block or deflect the punches hitting him as if he was a straight punching bag. Joker fell to the floor and was caught between the wall and the dirty ass toilet. He tried to crawl under the metal bed to avoid the fists of fury crashing hard against his body. Harlem was so caught up in putting in work on Joker that he didn't even hear the emergency alarm going off over the intercom alerting all guards that something was popping off on C-block in cell 124.

"I'll kill you, you bitch ass nigga!" Harlem screamed as he continued to stomp out the kid whose face was now puffy as hell and bleeding badly, and was doing his best to curl up into a tight ball, and screaming like a chick yelling for help. Harlem blacked out on psycho mode, and didn't stop until he was snatched up off him by two burly guards. Harlem then immediately turned his anger and aggression towards the guards and began tussling and beefing with them.

Joker was laying still on the floor unconscious in a puddle of his own blood. On the way out of the cell Harlem kicked a defenseless Joker in the face, causing more of his blood to splatter up against the cell walls. Harlem was super charged up and didn't give a fuck. It was what it was. In his eyes Joker knew that there was stupid smoke on deck, and that madd niggas from the Northside was looking and waiting for his ass. He should have been ready, but he found out the hard way what happens when you take niggas lightly, and write a check that your ass can't cash.

The COs dragged Harlem to the center of the cell block where they cuffed his hands and put security chains on his feet. The whole block was spazzin', all the prisoners was kicking their doors, calling the COs bitches, and yelling murderous threats at them.

All of a sudden the whole block got madd quiet, and you could hear what sounded like a bunch of wild horses running towards the block. When the block door opened you could see about twenty-five members of the Special Response Team, and they were dressed in full riot tactical gear, equipped with stun guns, pepper spray and large security screens, looking like giant aliens ready for war. Immediately they flooded the block in unison like roaches, and ran up on cell doors aggressively, barking orders and covering the little window on the cell doors with a piece of black vinyl, blocking their view from what was going on.

Superintendent Lexington, who ran the prison, was the only one not dressed to kill. He had on his usual everyday, drabby ass suit and tie hook up, and his ever present mean, red freckled faced mug. He walked over to where Harlem was being restrained and surrounded by COs, and knelt down to where his face was being pressed against the cold cellblock floor by a tactical team member's knee.

"I told you not to start any of your bullshit in my jail, asshole! Now tell me what part don't you remember or understand?" he said screaming as his words mixed with spit slammed against the side of Harlem's crunched up face.

"Fuck you! And get your racist ass ugly face out of mine, and stop fucking spitting on me!" Harlem said through gritted teeth.

After hearing that, one of the guards put his gloved hand around Harlem's throat and squeezed tightly. "Now that's not the way you talk to the boss, now is it, punk?" the officer who was in charge said.

"Man, suck a dick! You grimy motherfucker! Take these fucking cuffs off, and I'll show your bitch ass how real shit can get, you fucking coward! Shit, it takes a hundred of you weak bitches to handle one of me. All you faggots know how to do is beat up on inmates when their hands are cuffed with your scared-to-death ass."

"From the looks of things, it looks like you're the one who's the bitch, nigga. And if for some reason that inmate dies from his injuries, your black ass will be spending the rest of your natural life in a cage like the dog you are, you stupid dummy!" Superintendent Lexington said with a happy and devious look on his face.

"Man, ain't nobody gives two fucks what happens to that scram. He deserves everything he got coming to him! If that nigga dies, he die! You niggas can't break me! Cause North Side runs deep in my blood. And niggas like us are built Ford tough!" Harlem answered spitting blood out of his mouth that splattered the Superintendent's shiny, grey shoes with red speckles.

At that the officers got more aggressive, squeezing the handcuffs crazy tight. The pain was so out of this world that against his will Harlem let out a scream! When the prisoners heard him scream, and knew what they were doing, they started banging on their cells and kicking their doors again, wildin' out, calling the Superintendent a bitch and a hoe.

"Take this maggot piece of shit to the hole," the Superintendent ordered his Sergeant.

It was standard procedure to take all inmates to medical to be evaluated for injuries and their mental state before placing them in solitary confinement where the cells were soundproof. There was no physical contact with other prisoners. It was that ill, and designed to make you flip your lid, especially if you stayed there for crazy amounts of time. Madd niggas, who were tough on the block or on the tiers, folded and got soft in seg, and tried to hang themselves.

"Sir, what about medical?" Sergeant McDonald asked.

"I said the fucking hole and if you can't understand my English maybe you should return my stripes, Sergeant!" he said forcefully and with contempt.

"Yes, Sir," he answered nervously as he and three other officers snatched Harlem off the floor, and began carrying a kicking and fighting Harlem out of the block. They were pulling his cuffed arms apart like they were trying to detach them from his shoulders. The pain shot all through his body.

While the move team was extracting Harlem, Superintendent Lexington paced up and down the cellblock screaming and threatening the inmates who were locked behind cell doors.

"If you inmates keep banging on my fucking doors and making noise in my jail, I'll lock this block down indefinitely and you can spend the whole fucking summer there! Don't forget it's 90 degrees plus outside, which means those cells can get pretty hot and toasty, especially with no air condition! This is not the fucking Hilton Hotel. It's jail and you bastards are criminals! Believe me, I can make it a lot worse. Keep fucking with me and my staff and you will be in those cages sweating like slaves!" At that the banging slowed down.

"That's what I thought. You're all cowards and fake gangsters. Peterson, this block is locked down until further notice," he said heading back through the door on his way out of the block.

Superintendent Lexington used to be a Captain at the State Prison in Walpole. He was very hard on prisoners, and felt that lawbreakers deserved no mercy, no special treatment, no nothing. While Union Rep, he fought the Department of Correction to get rid of all TVs and radios, and felt that commissary and visits should be taken out of the system. He even went on Channel 5 trying to get public support. When he saw that wasn't going to happen he resigned and went into local politics for a while. He figured if he got elected he would then have the power to make the changes he felt were needed to punish criminals correctly. With no luck in the political arena, he got the position of Superintendent at Roslindale from Governor Patrick where he basically had his way.

On the way to solitary confinement, the guards did what they usually did when dealing with a rowdy nigga, and made a routine stop in what they called the "Midas Room." It was the COs old work out room. It deliberately had no cameras, and was under no type of surveillance. They brought prisoners there who they felt needed an ass whooping and an attitude adjustment. There they went bananas on Harlem beating him so bad that he passed out.

When he woke up he found himself in a smothering hot small concrete room, with a low light, naked and in four point restraints strapped down to a metal slab that was positioned in the center of the cell. He was beaten so bad and in so much pain, his entire body felt like a giant toothache. There was nothing else he could do, but try to rap himself to sleep to escape the pain. ❑

CHAPTER THREE
Back On The Block

HARLEM'S JORDANS HIT THE PAVEMENT hard as he stepped outside his building at the North Common Projects. His hood was on the North Side of Lowell, and was considered the most dangerous hood in the city. Harlem was born and raised on this battle ground and did madd dirt, and watched a lot of crazy shit happen on its gritty, unmerciful streets. These projects were extra wild, a place where drugs, gangs and violence ran rampant 24/7, and poverty was a lifestyle born into. It was nothing to see someone laid out dead from an overdose, with their pockets sticking out like rabbit ears, or to have a front row seat watching someone being shot, stabbed or beaten to death, or a fiend with swollen hands leaning against a telephone pole, nodding with tracks as long as the B&M Railroad running up and down his arms and neck, planning his next robbery. Or a kid about the age of thirteen standing on the corner looking up and down the street waiting for a cutty, Five-0 or a rival, with a bulge from the butt of a huge gun stuffed inside his waist. It was one of those type places that if you didn't live there, it was best to not go there, cause niggas was hungry and thirsty, and would eat you alive.

Harlem was madd hyped to be home. After seven years locked up, not much had changed. Niggas and chicks were doing the same shit they were doing before he left. It was like time had stopped on the block.

Harlem had a tight grin on his chocolate colored face, with cornrows in his hair which were a few days old, but at night he kept them wrapped in his du-rag so they were still on point. He had planned on getting a dope taper from Jayden's Fresh Cutz on Merrimack Street, and then go to Ty's Braids N Things on Adams Street to have them hook up his braids. He had heard that Ty's, a new joint in the hood, had African women over there who got it in on some exclusive shit when it comes to hooking a nigga's knot up. Every time he planned to go through, he always got out of the Studio too late. But he knew that was a for sure move he was gonna make as soon as he caught a break from hustling, and trying to get his money right, so that he could buy more studio time to finish his mix tape. He had spent madd time in lock up writing crazy raps, and practicing his rhyming skills. Nothing in life was more important. He was determined on becoming the first Rap Star out of the Mill City.

It was hot out, plus crazy muggy. It felt like the sun had the hood in a bear hug. At nine in the morning the hood was not fully bumping as usual. The projects usually came alive in the afternoon, when it was cooler. The only ones out now was drug dealers, dope fiends and crack heads who were trying to get their wake up by catching someone slipping, and then relieving them of their dough.

Faze, the neighborhood wino, was in his usual spot, sitting on a bench drinking a pint of vodka, what he considered breakfast for champions, and watching the hood which was his reality TV. Faze was his pimp name. His real name was Jeffrey Corey Courtney. He was a hood legend who at one time resembled Denzel Washington. Now, he was madd skinny and bald, and he looked like he was shrinking on a daily basis. Back in the days, his pimp hand was tight. He had eleven hoes at one time, and traveled all across the country getting money. Hood talk was that he had once been a millionaire, but when he lost his mother he blitzed, got broke and lost himself. Mrs. Courtney was his whole world, and when her world ended so did his. He came back to Lowell from the West Coast to bury his mom, and ended up staying. He started drinking, and started slipping heavy, and losing a piece of himself daily.

Everybody had love for him and would look out for him, especially the old heads that knew he was a good nigga, and had good game when it came to the chicks. The young heads heard about him, and every once in a while he would stop one of them and get them to buy him something to drink. In return he'd slice them off a piece of game. They say he may have forgotten madd shit, but one thing he never forgot was that the game was supposed to be sold not told.

Harlem peeped a few baby mamas he knew pushing their strollers towards Market Basket. They was trying to fill up their refrigerators by spending their monthly allotment of food stamps, which never seemed to be enough.

Right across the street in front of his building was a group of women standing outside of the Mercier Center with their shorties in tow. They were waiting for the gypsy bus that would take them and pick them up from the surrounding prisons where they went to visit their baby daddies and loved ones for a cool fee that wouldn't fuck up their pockets any more than they already was.

Harlem's nigga, Serious, had started this business when he touched down out of Norfolk Prison, after wrapping up a seven to ten year sentence. He saw that many niggas wasn't getting no love on the visiting tip. Their baby mamas always blamed their no show on transportation, and the fact that so many prisons were way out in the boondocks, madd far away from the hood.

So when he got out he did his one-two, and got on his grown man shit stacking up enough bread to give birth to this business. Not only as a way to get money, and pay his own bills, but to help the homies locked down to see their kids. For in the hood it was a rare thing for a kid to see or even know who the fuck their father is. That's why most say when you ask them about their father, they say it's the streets that raised me, so the streets is my dad.

Harlem crossed the street to hit up Paco's, the neighborhood bodega owned by a cool ass Puerto Rican homey who grew up in the neighborhood, and looked out for niggas on the credit tip not charging interest to grab a pack of Newports and a Mountain Dew. Harlem had been trying to put the brakes on smoking, cause it was definitely slowing him down. Not to mention at $10.00 a pack, expensive as hell. Shit, the tobacco company was sticking and charging niggas up like a Duracell battery. Harlem remembered his last beef with a kat from the South Side, and how he almost got dusted because after a few minutes he was running out of breath. After that bad performance he decided it was time to say deuces to smoking.

But lately, his stress levels were off the chart. Not only worrying about his mom and her up and down problems with drugs, and the drama with his girl Lauren's insecurities, but also all the bullshit he had to put up with and go through dealing with his fucked up probation officer.

Harlem checked his reflection in the window outside of Paco's to make sure his gear was on point. He had on a "Black Lives Matter" T-shirt, that this chick he met online from the movement gave to him, a pair of fatigue khakis and black Jordans, and his ever present black Jordan backpack full of his mixtapes slung on his shoulders.

He peeped an unmarked brown Taurus sitting across the street from his building trying to hide in the cut between two cars looking very suspect, and standing out like a sore thumb, especially for someone like him who had a sixth sense when it came to Five-O, he could basically smell when popo was around. Harlem looked at them and laughed and pointed at them yelling "One time is in the hood," so that everyone out trying to make moves would know they were there in the cut weighing niggas luck.

Shit had been hectic on the block. It seemed niggas had lost their minds. In fact, all across the city shit had been poppin' off. The Lowell Sun and the Boston Herald both have been reporting on what they called "senseless violence and murders on the streets of Lowell", with the newest wave of violence claiming twenty-seven lives in gang related shootings across the city. The latest casualty had been an innocent five year old boy who was sleeping in his bed when a gang gun fight jumped off on 6th Street, and ended with two bullets flying through his second floor window, hitting him in the stomach and in the head. That brought crazy heat to the Centreville section of the city, where the Bridge Street Bombers gang ruled the streets, prompting the Mayor and Police Chief to issue a curfew of 9:00 pm for anyone under the age of twenty living in the city's high risk drug and gang communities.

Shit was jumping off heavy on the streets of Lowell. The fucked up thing was all the victims were all under the age of seventeen. The Lowell Sun credited the increase of violence and murder due to the fact that not only was it summer, and when the temperature goes up so does the violence, the article suggested another key factor had to do with the recent release of numerous gang members that had went to prison for what the city had deemed the worst gang violence in its history. It was a war between the North and South Sides; a beef that started over a drive-by that took the life of Napoleon Rodriquez, a well-known figure high in the ranks of the North Common Fives. It was his murder that had set off a crazy bloodbath that had left thirty-two people dead.

Now some of those who had went to prison for their participation in that street war were being released, and returning to their communities and getting up with their respective gang factions. The recent gang wars were a direct result of the city's gangs jockeying for position as lead distributors in the city's lucrative drug trade, which was out of control. The Lowell Sun headlines barked that there was already twenty-seven murders, all senseless and it was only the second week of summer, which gave an overview of what to expect for the remaining of the summer. Many in the community blamed all the violence and murders on bad policing and the Government's fake ass war on drugs, mixed with an obvious lack of concern or interest by city officials who seemed to care less how many murders took place, especially since it was the minority community that were killing each other, and it stayed in those low poverty neighborhoods.

The minority community residents and activists, headed by a group called "The Mothers of Murdered Children" were very upset and vocal about the blood of their kids washing the streets of Lowell, and they protested by bringing their concerns to the front door of City Hall calling out the Mayor and City Officials accusing them of taking a lackadaisical approach to the blood of their children being spilled with no disregard. Even Reverend Al Sharpton came to Lowell to march and join the protesters calling for action and results, or the immediate resignation of the Mayor and his cronies. Their complaint was that if it had been White children who were being murdered, the whole entire Police Force plus the National Guard would have flooded the city, and would already have the murders solved; and the perpetrators already indicted and tried, and sitting inside of a concrete cell at the State's maximum prison in Walpole with a life-without-parole sentence. That's how fast justice moved when the victims are White. But since it is Black lives being lost, the wheels of justice were on a snail's time.

Harlem lit a bogey, checked his G-Shock and saw that it was 9:28 AM. He had thirty-two minutes to meet with his probation officer. He knew he had to be on point because dude was trying to fuck with him, and catch him slipping so he could violate his probation, and send him to Billerica House of Correction for eighteen months, for what he called affiliating with gang members and felons.

On his last time in front of the Judge, Mr. Nixon, his PO, brought this claim to the Judge as his basis for wanting to surrender Harlem. The Judge asked Harlem about it and Harlem told the Judge in his community all there is is pimps, prostitutes, drug dealers, gang bangers and criminals, so how could he not be around felons and gang members, if that's all he surrounded with, and that even his own mother and father both are drug addicts and felons with long ass records?

The Judge held him for second call giving him time to take his case under consideration. He decided to release him, and not lock him up because all his urinalysis tests had come back clean since he'd been out. Harlem didn't smoke weed, but he definitely smoked K2 like it was going out of style, and when he was chopping up work and bagging it he wore gloves to avoid the shit getting into his pores and system.

Feeling like Harlem got a break he didn't deserve, his Probation Officer put a full court press on him sweating him big time trying to find reason to knock him out the box. So Harlem moved differently, keeping his hustle on volume low and working a couple of days a week for his Uncle's moving company.

Harlem reached into his pocket and pulled out a tiny vial of Visine, and put drops into the corner of each red eye. When he got to Middlesex Street down by the homeless shelter where his mom worked he saw the brown Taurus pass him with both occupants clocking him hard. Harlem picked up his pace for he didn't want to be late and give his PO any reason to fuck with him.

After lighting another Newport he noticed the Taurus now with flashing lights and blaring siren coming straight at him jumping crazily onto the sidewalk, and cutting off his path stopping him right in front of the Registry of Motor Vehicles.

Both cops jumped out of the car simultaneously with guns drawn barking orders for him to put his hands up. They grabbed him and threw him hard up against the back of the car. The Black Cop held him down against the car while the White Freckled Faced Cop began rummaging through his pockets placing the contents on top of the hood of the cruiser.

"Damn bacon people! What's the problem? What did I do? Don't tell me you're stopping me for being a BMW (Black Man Walking)," Harlem said sarcastically.

"Oh, so you got jokes," the White Cop responded still searching his pockets and backpack desperate to find something.

"Nah, I ain't got no jokes. From the looks of things it's the Lowell Police Department that's got all the jokes," Harlem stated humorously.

"You think you're so cool and slick like we don't know you're still running with them North Side punks. You know, Mr. Valentine, since you've been out of prison there's been a lot more shootings. And guess what, asshole? All you scum are going down, and I mean hard. If I were you, I'd pack up and get out of Dodge because this city don't want your kind here," he said dumping out the backpack with mixtapes slamming against the hood of the car.

"Yo! Be careful with those CDs! That's my music and my life right there," Harlem said with a very sincere tone.

"Hey, Johnson, looks like we got one of those fucking MTV Rappers," he said to his partner, laughing.

"That's for sure, and one day you will see my name in bright lights and my handsome ass face on TV. Bet your kids will be riding my dick, and reciting my songs word for word. I mean you do know that 70% of all rap music is purchased by White kids?"

"What the fuck you say about my kids?" the White Cop said angrily and confused.

"Nothing. Just one day I will be your kid's favorite rapper."

"Shit, my kids don't even listen to that garbage. How about your kids, Officer Johnson?" he stated, looking at his partner, waiting for answer.

"Nope, not at all. Not in my house. Shit, you can't even understand what the hell they're saying," Johnson said chuckling.

"I'm going to tell you one more time. You're not wanted in this city. In fact, you never were wanted. So do everyone a favor, yourself included, and take your show on the road. Shit, go to Lawrence. You'd fit right in. They like low livers over there," he said seriously.

"Nah, think I'll stay here. I love Lowell. Besides if I wasn't here you wouldn't have nothing to do, but sit inside of Top Donuts, and stuff your faces with crème donuts. Shit, it's an epidemic. Cops all across the country are dying from getting so disgustingly fat that they are burst at the seams. So me being here is actually a pretty good deal for your health," Harlem said smiling.

"Well, we are tired of your bullshit in our city. People are afraid to come outside, and it's bad for tourism, which means bad for the economy. And to be honest, I could give two fucks if you all kill each other. It would make my job easier. But when it's innocent people that have nothing to do with your lifestyle getting caught in the crossfire, that's when I have a problem with it. And that's when I'm all up in your ass like a fucking enema."

A UMass Lowell cruiser pulled up, and rolled down his window. "You guys alright?" he said looking at Harlem as if he knew him, but couldn't recollect how or where from.

"Yeah, we're good. Just trying to help this young man with travel plans, and finding another city that best suits his purposes," he said with a "you know what I mean" smile. With that, the UMass Lowell Police pulled off.

"Your city?" Harlem questioned.

"That's right boy, our city," the Black Cop said standing there with an ill grill on his face, staring hard at Harlem with a look of utter disgust.

"Yo, can you do me a solid? Whatever you stopped me for, can you get it over with? I gotta be at the courthouse ASAP to check in with my probation officer. And can you stop breathing that pork filled breath on me! I'm allergic to it, and about to throw up Captain Crunch all over your new uniform," Harlem said putting his hand on his mouth like he was about to vomit.

"Spread the word, idiot. Tell all your fucking loser friends we are going to keep harassing all of you, and we are going to catch you. That's if you don't kill each other first. I'm telling you, even if I have to plant shit on you to get it done I will. You all are tearing this city apart. Citizens are complaining to the higher ups, who are complaining to us, and guess what? Shit rolls downhill," the white cop said.

"Yeah, whatever. Are you done? Cause I gotta bounce, and if you're really worried about crime, maybe you should go down to the Police Station and to City Hall. Cause that's where the biggest criminals are, by the dozens," Harlem said shaking free of the black cop's grip.

"Wise guy, huh? Just remember. This is our city, and we intend on cleaning it up and taking the trash out. There's no way a bunch of wannabe gangsters are going to have this city under siege," the white cop said resting his hand on the butt of his holstered gun, and gripping his nine millimeter tightly.

A crowd had formed out in front of the local businesses watching what was going on. Some had their cell phones out taking photos and videoing the altercation. Maybe they would catch another Rodney King moment.

Harlem lifted both his hands up and said "Don't shoot!" with a big smile on his face.

"Hey, you guys better get out of the sun. Didn't they teach you at the Police Academy that pork turns into maggots if it stays in the sun too long? For real, google it," Harlem said with a serious attempt to not laugh.

The Black Cop pushed Harlem away from the car.

"Get the fuck out of here, you fucking maggot nigger. It's niggers like you that make good black people look bad. Your mother should of used a clothes hanger when she found out she was pregnant with you," the Black Cop said seriously.

"Speaking of your mom how is that crack head whore doing? She must be clean, because I don't see her out here walking up and down the street trying to find a dick to suck so she can smoke crack," the White Cop said, smiling trying to antagonize Harlem.

"Have a nice day, Uncle Thomas. I mean your name is Thomas, isn't it?" Harlem said looking at the black cop's badge as he turned, and headed towards the courthouse with his middle finger in the air singing Lil Boosie's "Fuck Tha Police." ❑

CHAPTER FOUR

SITTING AROUND A WALNUT TABLE in a small room filled with boxes and bottles in the basement of the restaurant were four men representing different types of power in the city. But together they formed the Commission, an association that had a blueprint to take over the large scale operation of major drug and gun distribution throughout the city of Lowell and Middlesex County.

At the head of the table, governing the conversation, was Chief Ryan, a heavy chested man with greying hair and horn rimmed glasses. He was puffing on his Cuban cigar savoring the taste before blowing a cloud of smoke across the room. Also present was City Councilor Tran, a small quiet and mild mannered man who was in his second term representing the city and Asian Community. The Yellow Dragon, located on School Street across from 4M's Variety, was his restaurant. The other two men were friends of his who he had decided would be valuable in the implementation of their plan.

"So gentlemen, if anyone doesn't have any questions pertaining to the orchestration of our blueprint, anything at all to add that has not already been discussed that will assist us in immediately putting our plan into operation, this meeting is adjourned. And we all can go back home to our wives, and call it a day."

The men rose from their chairs, and ended the meeting like they did all meetings with the secret handshake of the Commission. The two younger men headed down the dark hallway out through another door that led to the laundry mat that was a couple of doors down from the restaurant entrance. The Chief and City Councilman sat back down.

"Well, my friend, we are about to make tons of money. Soon we'll be able to sit back, and retire to Florida, and buy a nice big house right between the beach and golf course, sipping martinis and living the life of Riley," the Chief said, smiling hard.

"Yes, yes. It's a beautiful plan, big guy," Councilor Tran said in agreement.

"Beautiful? That's all you think it is?" he said looking at Tran as if he missed something.

"No, my friend it's more than that! It's a multimillion dollar plan, and I'd rather have multi millions than beautiful any day!" he said laughing.

"Right! You're so right, big guy," Tran agreed, nodding his small head up and down.

Chief Ryan had been the Chief of Police of the City of Lowell for five years now. He came from a family heavily involved in Law Enforcement. His grandfather was a cop, and had risen through the ranks to become Lead Detective in the city, retiring after twenty-seven years of service. His dad was also a cop, and had died in the line of duty. He had been investigating a suspected human trafficking ring that smuggled young girls into the states for purposes of prostitution. Two years into the investigation, right when he was about to bring all his evidence to the Middlesex District Attorney, and gain indictments, he was found shot in the head three times with eleven more throughout his body on Bowers Street in the Acre section of the city. There were no leads, and the murder has never been solved.

Chief Ryan served on the City Council for two terms before being assigned as the Chief. As a City Councilman there was rumors throughout his whole term about his alleged involvement with shady characters, and back room business dealings with the city's underworld. However, nothing ever came of the accusations. He and his wife Beth had two children, a son, John, named after him, and a daughter named Meagan. John had died in a deadly car accident on Rte. 110 on his way back from his fiancée's house in Methuen after a birthday party.

Meagan, his 19 year old, was his heartbeat and heartache at the same time. Somehow she got caught up in the wrong crowd at Lowell High, and became a heroin addict despite all their efforts of intervention by him and his wife, Beth. They had already lost one child, and couldn't stand the thought of losing another.

Chief Ryan met Tran at the Mayor's Breakfast, an annual get together put on by the city to familiarize all those who work in local politics with each other. They both loved golfing and gambling, and were diehard fans of the Patriots. In fact, it was on one of their outings to Foxwoods that the Chief shared his plan with Tran. They saw an opportunity to make their financial dreams come true. The plan was to utilize the city's gangs as pawns to move their product. They felt that since there were four major gangs operating in the city in very strategic positions, they would have the great opportunity to control and distribute throughout the whole city. The goal was to get the major gang, the North Common Fives, to introduce their product which would be given to them uncut and more pure than anything out there on the market; which would knock the competition out of the box, and give them a chokehold on the clientele. They felt they were not hurting anyone since the gangs were already in the drug selling business, and all they were doing was taking advantage of a great opportunity. Shit, everyone knew that the war on drugs had proven to be a waste of time, and the government was not able and was unwilling to stop the flow of drugs no matter how much money or manpower they used. It seemed that every time they would lock up one drug dealer before they even got him to the police station, there was another dealer already standing in his place.

Chief saw Tran as the only person he could trust. He had already secured Tran's loyalty by using his power, position and connections to get Tran and members of his family liquor store licenses, and also licenses to sell liquor in their restaurants, and even helped them secure property to build an Asian Mall on Branch Street, across from Roberto Clemente Park which was taken over by the Asian Community. Tran didn't know then that he had made a deal with the devil.

Tran's nephew, Bonz, ran with the AM, (Asian Mafia) a well-established and powerful organization known for their ruthlessness. They were involved and controlled the numbers, prostitution, and gambling houses all over the city. In fact Bonz and a few of his homies were caught up in a counterfeiting ring that was making thousands upon thousands selling counterfeit money, licenses, ID's and green cards.

When it came to making money and orchestrating a plan, Bonz had the knack for making things happen and using the right people in the right places. In order for their plan to work, they needed Bonz's skill, and it was up to Tran to convince his nephew to play a part on the Commission's team.

"Oh shit, look what time it is. I am due to speak at UTEC's Annual Fundraiser. Well Tran, don't forget we got that city meeting next week in the chambers. Will you have an answer for me by then?" Chief Ryan asked looking at his watch.

"Yes, I'm hoping. Actually, I will see my nephew over the weekend. I believe he will recognize the opportunity to make lots of money, and come aboard. Also, Chief, have you decided which way you're going to vote?" Tran said gathering papers from the table, and getting them ready for the shredder.

"Well, it would be more beneficial to us if we placed our vote behind Deleon as well as persuade others to do so as well. Mr. Deleon has some very strong ties in the Dominican community, especially in

Lawrence, that we may be able to capitalize on in the very near future. You have to remember, that little city has major top level drug connections across the world. We would be wise to affiliate with him."

"Yeah, I agree. I see your point."

"I gotta get going. Don't forget to talk to that nephew of yours," Chief reiterated, walking out the door.

"I'll take care of it. You have a good time at the Fundraiser don't worry about a thing. I got my end covered. My nephew is a smart man, one thing he understand more than anything else is opportunity and money." ❏

CHAPTER FIVE

HARLEM WAS CHILLIN' in the projects, sitting in front of his building trappin' with his best friend ColdWorld, Mingo, and a few of his boys. They were smoking, and waiting on custies to pull through. It was the first of the month which meant fiends were getting their crazy checks, so there was dough to get, and they didn't want to miss one play.

"Yo, hurry up with rolling that blunt, Kizz, with your slow ass. What the fuck's wrong with your fingers, nigga? You got arthritis or something? Shit. You never put in on the weed, always want to smoke, and now on some turtle shit with the rolling," Mingo said, standing there madd impatient, playing with his dreads.

"Shit, you ain't lying, Mingo. I thought we was gonna wake and bake, not wait and bake" Kilo said taking the bottle of Henney out of the bag.

"Yo, ColdWorld, we gotta turn up, and get this dough. bro. I'm trying to get in the studio ASAP, and put this other mixtape together, cause the hood is on deck seriously waiting and anticipating. I'm not trying to be out here on this level of the game trapping for life, my nigga. This hand to hand shit is little nigga shit. I don't want to be stuck in this shit forever. Think about it, my nigga," Harlem said pointing to the projects around them.

"There's got to be more to life than this, and I want it. All niggas do is smoke weed, sling rocks, beef and kill each other; while other niggas are getting their dough up, investing, and getting rich. It's like we got the plan, but slept on the formula that would take us to where we want to go. And that's not to the front doors of the jail house neither.

"Yo dawg, what's gotten into you? Oh, I get it. You been talking to crazy ass Serious, who all of sudden got all the answers to this struggle niggas are going through out here in these streets hustling, and trying to creep on a come up. Shit, what fucking Ghetto Bible he cop his knowledge from?" Mingo said laughing, and reaching out to give daps to his younger brother Murda, who was sitting on the hood of Mingo's Acura talking with some Spanish chick, who lived in the Belvidere section of the city, which was the turf of their mortal enemies The 460's.

"Yo, my nigga, don't sleep on Serious for real. He really be spittin' that knowledge at us to try to get our heads tight, and put us onto some new and improved shit. He may sound like he trippin' to you, but he be keeping it a buck. Look how he's moving, my dude. Shit, that nigga went from holding a gun in his hand to holding a business plan. He out here doing his one-two. You can't hate or throw shade on that. Ever since that nigga got out of prison, his third eye has been wide open, and he been on some getting money the legal way type shit. It's you, nigga, that got it twisted, and can't see what he be talking about, cause you small minded, and don't know jack about wisdom, knowledge and understanding.

Shit, you all are cool with this project living shit, banging and fighting niggas in the street and roaches trying to sleep. I never got into this trappin' shit to stay. It was just a launch pad to get my dough correct, and put me on the path to this rap and making hits, shit. It was about making my dreams come true. All I think about is rocking stages and seeing the world, and that's a double fact," Harlem said with his head looking up and down Salem Street checking for popo or a custy.

A fiend came walking towards them. She was an old head that at one time was on top of her game and doing her thing-thing. She used to be a fly ass chick who had her own boutique, and was jeweled the fuck up with a fresh ass Benz and a fly crib up in the Highlands. Now all she all she does is run up and down Westford and Appleton Streets looking raggedy and smoking crack.

Her man, Pump, was that dude that had the whole city on lock at one time, and put in madd work until he got bagged for a body, in a drug robbery gone bad. Niggas had ran up in his crib trying to take his shit, so he did what any real nigga would do, and blasted one of the chumps.

The fiend had on a dirty "I Love Mill City" T-shirt and a hand full of crumbled up dollars that she handed to Mingo, who handled the money as if he could catch some type of virus from them.

"Bitch, get your nasty ass out of here, you only got seventeen dollars. Niggas ain't taking no shorts" he said throwing the crumbled money at her, with it hitting her and falling onto the ground. Kilo and Murda started laughing hard.

"Come on, young blood, I always cop my shit from you all. Shit, I'm loyal to spending money with you niggas, even when the shit ain't that good and cut with too much baking soda I still come through, and spend," she begged, looking at them like they were crazy.

Harlem walked over and picked the money up off the ground, straightening it all out, and handing it back to her. "How you been, Porche? Thought you was done with this shit, and going to rehab," he said with much respect and concern.

"Yeh, I am. When? I don't got a clue. Things have been crazy complicated, but I'm definitely tired of this shit; especially when I'm getting disrespected by little niggas," she said eyeballing Mingo.

"Do that, Ma. You got a good head on your shoulders. You know I got madd love for you and your peeps, and I wanna see you get back to being the real you," he said turning to Mingo. "Yo, Mingo, let me see your work," Harlem said irritated.

Mingo reached into the back of his pants, and pulled out a plastic baggy filled with $40 dollar pieces, and handed the bag to Harlem with a confused look on his face. Harlem reached into the bag, and pulled out a handful of smaller plastic bags with crack in them, and gave them to Porche. She looked at Harlem surprised, with big eyes not sure what was going on or what to do next, so she stood there looking at the crack rocks and at Harlem, waiting for the punchline.

"Yo, Mingo apologize, fool nigga."

"For what?" he said looking at Harlem."Shit, if anything, she should be the one apologizing for not coming correct from the jump. These motherfuckers act like this shit don't cost us no dough. Ain't nobody told her to be a fucking crack head," he said matter of factly. You could see on his face, he was tight.

Harlem just looked at Mingo with an ill grill."Because I said so, nigga. What, you wanna try me, dawg?"

Mingo looked at Kilo and Murda, who were just trying to keep from bursting out because they knew Harlem was dead ass serious, and didn't want to irk the situation.

"Yo, my bad, Shorty," he said slowly and reluctantly.

"My nigga, don't ever treat her or anyone of our custies like that. We eating because of them. Next time you do something trippy like that, I'll be on your ass like flies on shit, and if I'm having a really bad day you just might be sipping your food through a straw, That's facts, bro. That shit ain't cool for business" he said handing the rest of the bag to Mingo.

"Go ahead, Ma. Go do your thing. That's yours on me, ok? How's Big D doing? Shit he should be wrapping up by now. Shit, he been down a minute."

"He good. He got about six months left. He called my mama's house last week."

"He still up in Shirley Max?" Harlem asked.

"Yeh, the class board shot him down, and wouldn't let him go to minimum because of his assault on COs two years ago."

"Yeh, I was up there with that nigga. He don't be taking no shorts at all. He be reppin' hard. Tell the nigga I said what up, and tell your mom I'll be by to hit her with a few dollars to send to him for his books, aiight?"

"Yeah I will," she said reaching out with the opposite hand to shake Harlem's. He ignored her hand, and reached out, and hugged her like a sister. She smiled showing rotten teeth.

"Harlem smiled."Go do you, and take care of yourself, and get your butt in rehab" he said turning back to Mingo.

"Nigga, let me put you on to something. When that chick was on point, and out in these streets hustling, trust me, dawg, a nigga like you couldn't tie her shoes. That chick got more game in her pinky than you have in your whole fucking body. And she's handled more money than you will see in your lifetime. So, you better act like you know, cause a chick like that can teach you a few things about getting bread in these streets, for real," Harlem said.

"That's a fact, dawg. Porche was that chick. Plus her bro is a real ass nigga. We fuck with that family hard. They from this hood originally, but when their mom got sick they moved to a more quieter place. But yeah, my nigga, if you or any of us knew what she knew about this drug game, we'd be caked the fuck up in this game. You can't treat niggas like shit. Fiend or no fiend, cause you never know," ColdWorld co-signed.

Turning back to the crew,"Like I was saying, there's gotta be more to life than this, and I'm at it. I don't know about ya'll niggas, but I want to be on top of the world."

Everyone was staring at Harlem like 'what the fuck just happened?' ❑

CHAPTER SIX

YOUNG M.A'S SONG OOOUUU, exploded out from the speakers filling the shop with a festive type atmosphere at Jayden's Fresh Cutz. Harlem was in the chair getting his shit right, when his cellphone vibrated in his pocket. It was Toy, his girlfriend, Lauren's sister. At first he was going to send it straight to voicemail, but decided to answer it.

"Yo," he answered in a drowsy ass voice.

"Harlem! Yo, dude! They just popped Mercedes at the Radisson in Chelmsford in an undercover prostitution sting. They flagged her on her backpage ad, and set her up, sending an undercover agent posing as a Trick to her room there."

"Shit! I told that chick she needed to slow her fast ass down just the other day."

Mercedes was Harlem's cousin. She had five kids, and was 30 years old. Her baby daddy was killed a year ago inside of Mill City Ballroom night club arguing over a chick. Being a single mother, Mercedes, hustled hard to keep food in her babies' stomachs and clothes on their backs. She was on Section 8, so that took care of them having a roof over their head. She had a tough ass life with her mother getting killed by one of her crazy ass boyfriends, who used her for a punching bag when Mercedes was seven. Ever since then, she has been raised and bouncing around from family member to family member. Mercedes and Harlem were madd tight and they always looked after each other no matter what they had that type of bond.

"So what's her bail?"

"$2500. They're holding her at the State Police Barracks in Andover. We're trying to get her out before she goes in front of the Judge, cause with her past record, shit might double. If you want, me and Liah will go scoop her up. I know how you don't like jailhouses,' she said with a quick laugh.

"Yeah, I got you. Give me about a half, I'm at the barber shop, I'll meet you at the crib."

"Ok, hit me up when you're there."

"Facts." ❏

CHAPTER SEVEN

"NAH, MS. VALENTINE, I can't do that. Harlem's my Dawg, and he would kill me if I sold you drugs," Kizz said trying to end the conversation.

"Listen baby, it ain't for me. It's for my homegirl that I work with at the Shelter. I'm just trying to keep money in the family, and at the same time look out for my girl. Shit, I know how it is to be fiending," Ms. Valentine said with a suspicious smile on her face.

"Well, your best bet is to tell homegirl to come through, and I will serve her. But I ain't got nothing for you. I wish you would stop sweating me bout this shit, real talk."

Mrs. Valentine was Harlem's mom. She looked madd good for her age. Everybody said she looked like Mary J. Blige a little bit. Over the years, she'd been in and out of drug programs, battling her addiction to crack cocaine. In fact, she lost Harlem to the Department of Child Services when he was five. Crack at one time had such a stronghold on her that she would do bugged out shit, like leave Harlem to drug dealers as collateral for drugs, until she was able to catch a trick, and sell her body to complete strangers to get money to pay them back, and get her son back from them. It was Harlem's grandmother, a God fearing woman, that would go to the Courts, and fight the system to get custody, while his mom was out in the streets smoking crack, and living in crack houses with whatever dealer had the crack at the time. His mom would get clean for a minute, then the next thing you knew, she was back to smoking and running the streets again. One day she was on a crazy six day crack binge, when she walked into the Lowell Five Bank with a note saying she had a gun, demanding the teller to empty her cash draw, and give her the money. As soon as she got it, she walked straight to a crack house on Merrimack Street, and was beaming up to Scottie.

She was so done, that the landlord who owned the building got a call from one of the tenants that a woman was running around in the hallways of the rooming house paranoid and hallucinating, butt naked, saying that people were trying to kill her, and chop her up into pieces. He called the police who went to the scene, and found an out-of-her mind Ms. Valentine on the dirty bathroom floor with a fork digging into her skin, claiming she was trying to take out the tracking device that the people looking for her had put into her.

They also found about $9,000 dollars scattered across the bathroom floor. The EMTs immediately took her to Lowell General Hospital for an evaluation. While there, the Lowell Police had discovered she was the suspect they were looking for from the robbery at Lowell Five a couple days before. So they went there and arrested her, and gave her a bedside arraignment. After a few days, she was medically cleared, released into the custody of the Middlesex Sheriff's Department, and brought to MCI Framingham to await her next court date. She ended up copping out to a three to five years sentence with three years' probation.

After serving half her sentence, she was paroled. She went into a drug program out in Falmouth to address her addiction issues. There she prepared to get custody of Harlem back, who had been living with her mom. Since then, she'd had a few minor slips, but nothing major. Now she'd been clean for almost thirty-eight months, and going to NA meetings at the Lowell House on Appleton Street, and working as a Placement Coordinator at the Shelter. Her and Harlem's relationship had gotten a lot better, although he was always clocking her, and to see if she was still fucking around on the low.

"So, you're really not going to sell me three for $100? Shit, boy, I used to change your shitty ass diapers, Kerry, and you treating me like this?" she said still trying to persuade him.

"Nah, like I said, Ms. V. I'm good with that. Dead ass, you're just wasting your breath with me. I'm just trying to figure out how I am going to tell my Dude his mom is back out here getting high on her bullshit again," he said uncomfortably.

"You're not going to tell him shit. You hear me? And like I told you, it isn't for me so there's really nothing to tell, right?" she said getting angry.

"Well, the only way I'll not tell him, is if your stop sweating and pushing up on me about this crack shit. What the hell happened? You were doing so good Ms. V. and Harlem was crazy proud of you for real," Kizz said adamantly.

"Nothing happened. I'm good, and we will just keep this between us. My Son don't need to know about this. I guess I will just tell my homegirl I couldn't get it," she said lying.

"Yeah you do that," Kizz said, knowing she was lying, cause he dealt with crackheads all day, every day, plus his own Mother was a crackhead, so he grew up watching it in living color, and knew when someone was on that shit. And Ms. V. had definitely started smoking again, and he knew when Harlem caught wind of it he was going to bug the fuck out. ❏

CHAPTER EIGHT

HARLEM WAS FRESH FROM THE BARBER SHOP, and was outside in their usual hangout, sitting on the benches in front of his building with his homies and some friends having a cookout. Mingo's girl Trish was cooking chicken, hamburgers and hotdogs on the grill while Mingo was hooking up the potato salad.

"Hey Harlem, you know your cousin Mercedes got bopped, and is in jail, right?" said a tall skinny model type girl dressed in a Pink Bathrobe and matching Nike Sandals, walking towards the cooler to snatch up a Heineken.

"Yeah, I'm hip. Toy hit me up, and told me. She's straight though. I'm about to have them go snatch her up," he responded, trying to get his mixtape to work. For some reason it just stopped, and became stuck inside of the CD player.

"Shit, let me hit that blunt, ColdWorld. Hey, what's up Kilo?" she said reaching for it out of ColdWorld's hands.

ColdWorld passed it to her with a crazy grin on his face. "Now be easy with my blunt, Diamond, you know your ass got weak lungs," he said smirking, trying not to laugh, and release the smoke in his mouth out too early. She hit it madd hard on some greedy shit, and immediately spit out the smoke mixed with saliva, and started coughing hard. "What the fuck kind of weed is this!?" she asked staring at the blunt in between her fingers, and holding it away from her as if it was about to blow up.

"It's that new death, Kush," ColdWorld said laughing.

They had mixed weed and K2 together which put them on tilt

ASAP. It was Kizz that started doing this, now they rolled up like that on a regular.

"Shit, it's the type of weed that will teach you to stop asking for something you don't ever put a dime into with your greedy ass," Mingo said laughing.

"Nah nigga, that better not be no Angel Dust or that fucked up K2 shit getting me all trippy and shit. Nah, I smoked that shit before with one of my homegirls, and the shit had me buggy. I'm not cool with smoking this shit. It taste like some crazy white boy type of high shit," she said handing the blunt back to ColdWorld.

Everybody started busting out and laughing at Diamond, even the lil shorties was all up in her business laughing. That shit had her feeling some type of way.

Lauren, Harlem's on again off again girlfriend, came out of the building with some packages of hotdog rolls and hamburger buns. She was twenty-four, and madd beautiful, with no kids. Everyone said she looked like Meagan Good. Her and Harlem grew up together, and knew each other since the second grade, and began kicking it in the ninth grade while they both were on the Lowell High Track Team. Their moms were get-high partners, and back in the day when they were running the streets smoking crack and hustling, people always mistook them as sisters. In fact, the first time their moms got locked up, it was together and for an armed robbery. They had ran into this Dominican trick from Lawrence who was a crazy ass freaky deaky nigga that had a strange sex appetite, and was a strong dope and coke connect that used to pay them drugs to do threesomes and other wild sex shit that only a chick on drugs would do.

One day, while smoking crack and tweeking hard at Motel 6 in Tewksbury, they came up with a crazy ass plan to beat him for his stash and dough. They met up with him and started freaking, and getting high with him at the Telly. The nigga was so zooted and wasted off of percs but wouldn't knock out. So they straight laced his drink with Seroquel which knocked him dead out as if he got hit with a punch from Micky Ward. While he was dozing, they went to his whip, and robbed him for a brick and a half a key of coke. They split the drugs and went on a madd run getting high and bugging out.

A few days later a twelve year old Lauren found her mom on the top of the roof of their building dead with a needle full of blood sticking out of her arm. The Department of Child Services snatched Lauren and Toy up and held them until they went to Dorchester to live with their aunt, and two years later they moved back to Lowell with their grandmother.

Harlem and Lauren's relationship was complicated. She was madd insecure, and always complaining about everything. When Harlem got locked up, she did look out and stand by him and visited him regularly, making sure he had bread on his books. But he also found out from Kizz that she was fucking some kat that she met on Instagram from Nashua, New Hampshire. He confronted her, and she kept it a hundred, and admitted it. They broke up, and it changed the very nature of how they kicked it with each other. When they did get together on some try-again shit, they were at each other's throats. She was always accusing Harlem of this chick and that chick because he never spent any real time with her. She felt she had been reduced to a booty call and that was it. Harlem told her yeah he was seeing someone else, and madly in love with his new chick. She wild out wondering who the new chick was, blowing his celly up like a madd deranged chick until he finally told her, his new wifey was his music thing, and that was the bitch that was getting all his extra time.

Toy pulled up in her Land Rover with Future's "Too Much Sauce" playing madd loud. All the little shorties started singing and dancing and throwing their hands up. When Harlem saw Toy pull up he snatched up his cup filled with Hennessy, and tipped it guzzling the rest to his face, and headed inside the building to his crib to get the bread for Mercedes' bail. Everyone was chillin', turning up, and having a good time when a black Yukon with dark tinted windows pulled around the corner off of Adams Street onto Salem Street, moving crazy slow.

When the truck got close, the back window rolled down, and the tip of a AK 47 Assault Rifle came out. That's when shit got critical, and all hell broke loose. Harlem was halfway up the stairs in the building when he heard the sound of a gun clacking, mixed with the sound of people screaming, and bullets hitting the walls and other objects. He snatched the 40 Cal off the back of his waist, and rushed back downstairs. By the time he exited his building, he saw everybody scattered all over the ground, and everything a straight fucking mess where a few minutes before niggas was getting it in on some cool summertime type shit.

He heard the screech of tires, and peeped a Black Yukon speeding away, turning right onto Decatur Street. Harlem ran behind it busting off shots with no luck. He put his heater back into his waist, and sprinted back to the cookout where people were crying, and getting up off the ground where they got low to avoid being hit. Shit was everywhere. The food and grill was tipped over with hotdogs, hamburgers and charcoal scattered on the grass. Harlem looked for Lauren and saw her and Toy kneeling down next to ColdWorld, who was laying on his back and not moving.

"Somebody call an Ambulance!" an older Spanish Woman, with a "Be A Buddy Not A Bully" T-shirt on, shouted out.

"Ahh shit, they hit my nigga!" Harlem said kneeling down, lifting ColdWorld's head off the ground. "Yo, my nigga! Wake up, breathe! Breathe my nigga!!" Harlem begged his homie.

"The Dispatcher said an Ambulance is on the way," Mrs. Hernandez, the next door neighbor, said from behind the screen door to her crib.

"Man, fuck the Ambulance! They never come to the hood on time. By the time we sit here waiting for them slow ass people, my nigga will have bled the fuck out. Yo, Toy! We going in your whip!" Harlem yelled impatiently.

"Lauren, you call Lowell General, and let them niggas know we coming, and to be ready," he said picking ColdWorld up, and carrying him to the Land Rover.

All the way to the Hospital Toy was complaining about all the blood everywhere inside her new car. "Shit, shut the fuck up Toy! Damn, our nigga laying here damn near bout to breathe his last, and all your selfish ass can think about is a fucking car!" Harlem said angrily. Toy was so tight about everything that she mashed on the gas pedal, and was driving so fast you would of thought she was trying to get away from the popo, or drag racing in the Indianapolis 500.

When they reached the hospital there was a few nurses and orderlies standing out in front of the Emergency Room entrance with a gurney and IV drip waiting for their arrival. ❏

CHAPTER NINE

CITY COUNSELOR TRAN WAS SITTING in the passenger seat of the money green Beamer smoking a blunt, and kicking it with his nephew, Bonz ,who was driving, and listening to his uncle put him on to the master plan of the Commission. He told Bonz that the role he would play was major, and necessary if they were to be successful, and that they could all potentially walk away from it financially secure if they played their cards right.

"So, you're saying that the drugs will be shipped to the United States inside the dead bodies of Cambodians, and that there would be no interference with Customs?" Bonz asked curiously.

"Correct. Through my resources we have established a contact in the government that will provide us with the documents that will allow any Cambodians who die, and have a multitude of family members who are Citizens of the United States, with the option of burying them over here for financial reasons. For it would be much more cost effective for the families as opposed to all family traveling back to Cambodia for funeral," Tran said looking at his nephew with a half-smile on his face.

"And how the hell will the drugs be taken out of the corpses? And who will do it? Cause that's not my thing. I ain't got no problem killing a motherfucker, but I'm not trying to fuck with no dead bodies, Unc," Bonz said looking at his Uncle with all sincerity.

"Relax. We got that all taken care of also. You remember my friend, Choum, whose wife works at City Hall and is good friends with your Mom? Well, him and his son, Arunny, have a funeral home on Westford St, and they will receive the bodies, and do all the dirty work of cutting them open and taking out the drugs for us, and then dispose of the bodies through cremation," Tran said matter of factly.

"Now, all you have to do is use the partnerships the Asian Mafia has already established with the gang leaders throughout the city, and disperse it to them, and let them break it down for their runners. As long as our numbers are solid and correct, that's the Commission's only concern. Your job is to manage the field, and play quarterback. We can all get our piece of the pie," Tran said.

"Be the Tom Brady of the drug game, huh? Sounds pretty good, Uncle. I'll talk to my people about it ASAP, and will give you a call in a few days. Our next meeting is on Saturday, so I will have an answer for you after the meeting. But I'm sure the top niggas will green light it, and be 100% down, especially when they see the potential and large profit margin. I know you're a great businessman, and would never steer me wrong. If you say this is well thought out, then your word is all I need. So as V.P. I could green light it myself, but out of respect, just let me run it by them, and make a few calls to set up some meetings with the leaders of the sets in the city. Now, pass my blunt. You been nursing it every since we got on the Connector," Bonz said laughing. ❏

CHAPTER TEN

HARLEM WAS WALKING BACK FROM THE STUDIO which was housed in the Saab Building on Central Street. He had been there most of the day lacing the tracks for his next mixtape. Shit went madd dope at the studio. His flow was tight, and he figured within the next week he would be finished with his 2nd mixtape. He was also scheduled to go on the Launchpad on 94.5 next week to create a buzz for his new shit. So much was going on around him that he needed to hit the studio. It was therapeutic, and helped him to relieve some of the stress he was dealing with. Later that night the whole clique was getting together to kick it about ColdWorld's shooting, and get all ears to the street to catch a clue on who was responsible for it. He knew that shit was going to get super turnt up and crazy in the next few weeks. ColdWorld was his brother from another mother. They knew each other since they were babies, and rode for each other hardbody. He wanted nothing but to see the niggas that did it suffer, Hannibal Lector style.

While walking down Fletcher Street he peeped the paramedics and police tending to a homeless woman laid out on the sidewalk, not moving. He recognized her as this older white chick named Cassie who came through once in a while to cop rock off him. Cassie and her man were boosters, so they would bring all types of stolen shit to him for the low price. Most days you would see her standing at the intersection of Dutton and Fletcher Street, holding a sign, and an empty coffee cup, hustling money from cars caught at the red light. He walked closer and heard the paramedic ask his partner for Narcan, which is used to reverse the effects of an overdose. Damn, another person overdosing on the garbage them out-of-town niggas be selling.

"What the fuck are motherfuckers putting in their heroin?" Harlem thought to himself. He walked off and down Adam Street rapping to himself. By the corner of Broadway and Adams Street he saw a familiar face, and stopped and hollas at him. It was Bonz, an Asian Kat he had met in Billerica House of Correction. They were runners on F-Pod together. One day some kats from Boston were about to jump Bonz on some bullshit bully shit, over a bet on the Patriots game. Harlem stepped in, and sided with Bonz, telling them he was going to ride with Bonz, and if they fucked with Bonz then they fucked with him and his team. Bonz was a solid dude. He did his bid right, and always handled his business, and was not afraid to beef with one or a hundred niggas. He was real like that, and Harlem liked that about him. After seeing niggas posted up behind Bonz, niggas thought twice about riding on him, and instead gave Bonz a fair one with one of their peeps, which was the wrong move because he ended up putting a niggas whooping on the kat. After that Harlem and Bonz became cooler than two flies sleeping on ice cubes.

"What's up Harlem?" Bonz said walking from across the street towards him, leaving a group of ready to die looking Asian kats standing on the porch of a fresh house, listening to Tupac, and playing dominos and drinking. But they stayed on point, and had their eyes cut to the side, watching Bonz and Harlem's interaction closely.

"Chillin' my nigga, you already?" Harlem said giving him daps. "Yo, when you get out my dude?"

"Man, shit. I stayed in that fucked up joint, Billerica, for two and some change waiting trial, and then once I blew trial, I had to go up State, and give them fools 4 years. I been home for about a year and a half now," Bonz said in a thick ass voice, that didn't seem to fit his body. He was short and weighed about a buck fifty.

"I been out for two and some change myself," Harlem said matter of factly.

"That's what's up. Shit, them fools ain't playing. You better try to stay off the radar, cause they quick to lock a nigga up out here, you know? Them Lowell Police ain't bullshitting, ya heard?"

"That's a fact. I'm already hip. Yo, you stay over there?" Harlem said pointing to a dope brown three family house across the street where the music was coming from.

"Yeah, that's the family's spot," Bonz said proudly.

"I hear that. Shit, that's a pretty dope spot."

"That's why we hustle, to have things, and live comfortable, you know?"

"True. Yo, let me get your math, so we can build sometime," Harlem said pulling out his IPhone.

"For sure. I gotta get my jack. It's in my car," Bonz said walking towards a money green BMW.

"This you too, dawg?" Harlem asked, admiring the whip that was sitting pretty in the driveway of the crib.

"Yeah, that's just one of my joints. I got a F150 truck also, but my girl got it. Shit, she love driving that more than my Beamer or the Audi I bought for her!" he said shaking his head.

"Wow, boy, you doing it like that?"

"Got to. Don't make no sense being in these streets hustling, if all you hustling for is a bag of weed and a pair of Jordans. That shit is uncool. If a nigga out here playing with his life, he might as well play big. Anything else is like hustling backwards.

Shit, you saw the prison yard full of kats who played small out here not respecting the game, and jeopardizing their freedom for crumbs. Now look at them. Them niggas is starving, and wearing Bobos and can't even afford a Ramen Noodle Soup from the prison commissary."

"Copy, my nigga. I'm feeling how you living. That's the type of shit

I'm trying to be on. Bout time I see a nigga who think like me. Yo, you gotta put me onto next level game, so I can blow, and get a fist full of dollars to invest in this rap shit. Cause I know with a little help, the rap world would be mine, and that's a double fact," Harlem said excitedly.

"I got you. Give me a call in a few days. I'm putting something major together that is worth crazy bread, and you can have a piece of the pie if you're ready to step your game up, cause ain't no half stepping in what I'm about to do. But if you're ready, then I got a boss's position for you that will allow you and your whole team to eat off of bigger plates."

"You already know. Shit, dawg, speed that, cause I need that," Harlem said excitedly.

"You can handle big shit, can't you? Cause I got an ugly connect, and a nonstop supply of that Brown and White," Bonz asked looking hard into Harlem's eyes.

"Yeah, I can make it happen for sure. We got the north side on lock, and they be coming through hard for that Brizzy too. The shit them niggas is selling now is putting mother fuckers in the grave. Shit is ugly out here. Niggas are madd stupid selling shit that is knocking niggas out. How the fuck you gonna kill off your money supply like that? You know what I'm saying, my nigga?" Harlem said looking perplexed, and shaking his head.

"Yo, you're right. That shit is bananas. I heard it's them out of town niggas. Don't stress. We about to end them niggas' career out here for real. Yo, you still listening to that nigga, Meek Mill?" Bonz asked smiling."Yo, I told you when we was locked that he couldn't fuck with that nigga Drake."

"Yeah, I peeped that now. He slippin' hard. Yo, can you believe he bagged Nicki Manaj?"

"Yeh, that's the word. Lucky ass nigga. Yo, Drake hit him with a knockout punch with that song "Back to Back." He asked that nigga Meek, "Is that a world tour or your girl's tour" shit talking bout shots fired." Bonz said making the sound of a gun firing.

"Yeah, he shit on him hard. I heard the beef on the Launchpad way back, then hit up the internet to keep with the latest. That nigga Meek is quiet, which is his best bet. Fucking with a nigga like Drizzy is not healthy for that nigga's career," Harlem agreed.

"Yo, your man Cheddar, the Asian kat from Lynn, was at the studio today putting in work. He sound madd nice with his flow. I was trying to get his man to hit me with some tracks so I could lace them."

"Yeah, he hit me up telling me he was coming to town. He will most likely pull show at my crib after he's done. That's my dude right there. I've been trying to get with him to invest some loot in him, but because of the grimy niggas he be rocking with, I haven't been able to lock nothing down with him. But yeah, the nigga is nice.

I got this nigga that just started working for a major record company in Cali, he a blood nigga, but shit, I think he would fuck with you and Cheddar. On some real shit, you two need to hook up, and put something down I could send to him."

"Shit, remember when we was up in ten block in Walpole, that nigga kept the whole tier entertained on rec status with his rapping. He had niggas sleeping during the day, and staying up all night on some bullshit," Bonz said laughing.

"Yeh, maybe me and that nigga could do something. I'll holla at him next time we bump heads at the studio. Yo, I gotta be out. I'm on my way to go check on my nigga laid up at Lowell General. I'll holla at you. Yo, hit me up on Instagram or the Book."

"No doubt. I'll do that. Give me till Friday. I'll have something lined up, and we can get together and build on it," Bonz said extending his hand for daps.

"No doubt. I also got something madd personal to holla at you about. A nigga may need some burners. Can you make it happen?"

"Just holla at me. We will talk all things important," Bonz said going back to where his boyz were on the porch.

Harlem was talking about copping some more firepower, so they could be ready for the payback. No doubt when they found the niggas, it was going to get ugly real quick, cause he was about to raise the death toll. He had his suspicions what crew did it, but without facts he couldn't move on them. He wondered if a past beef had been brought back to life. If his hunch was right, then it was about to be World War Three on the streets of Mill City.

Harlem was madd happy to have run into Bonz, and see the nigga doing his one-two, and on a grown man's grind. Shit, maybe they can chase paper together. By the looks of things, Bonz is eating well, and he wanted to sit at that table also.

He turned up Fletcher Street, and headed towards Lowell General Hospital to check on ColdWorld. Last night his nigga was still in ICU, unconscious, and in critical condition. Doctors were madd skeptical on whether or not he was going to pull through. In fact they gave him a 75 to 25 chance of pulling through, which he knew was fucked up odds. ColdWorld's mom, Ms. Rosado, along with the rest of his family kept a bedside vigil.

The Lowell Sun mistakenly reported that ColdWorld had been hit one time in what appeared to be a drug deal gone bad. But the truth was, there was no drug deal, and no one knew what the fucking reason was. He was shot three times, twice in the stomach and once in the face. One of the bullets was still lodged a centimeter away from a major artery. The Doctor who performed the operation felt to attempt to remove it would probably kill him. So, they left it untouched. ColdWorld, at nineteen, was too young to die. Too many he knew already died before their eighteenth birthday. The real fucked up thing was ColdWorld was due to start College in September at UMass

Lowell, and play ball for them.

His whole room was filled with his team and women from his mom's Church. They were considered the prayer warriors, and were known to get results from their prayers. It was like they had a special connection with the Man up above, because when they prayed Heaven made major moves for them.

All the homies that he rocked with came through to check on him, and to show support. Niggas that never prayed before, found themselves on bended knees reaching out to heaven to snatch up a Blessing.

Mingo and Ms. Rosado never saw eye to eye. In fact, any time ColdWorld got caught in a rough situation, or was arrested, she would blame it on him hanging around that bad ass boy. Mingo and his twin brother Murda were known in the hood to be crazy ass troublemakers. Growing up, no one wanted their kids to hang out with them. Them niggas quit school in the fifth grade, and was running around the hood wildin' when they were but yay high.

Inside the waiting room packed with his team, she went to get what seemed like her hundredth cup of coffee out of the vending machine, and talk in private to her Pastor. Ms. Rosado saw Mingo, and started going in on him, asking what he was doing there, and they got into a heated argument.

She blamed Mingo for her son being shot, and told him he was not welcomed at the hospital, and if he didn't leave, she would have security escort him out. Mingo was extra tight, and talked his shit. But before shit got a little extra, he bounced, feeling some type of way.

ColdWorld's pregnant girlfriend, Cake, who also grew up in the North Common Projects, was also rushed to the same Hospital. When they gave her the news about him being shot, upon hearing it, she passed out right in the Lowell Community Health Clinic where she worked. Her and ColdWorld were madd close, and had been one another's backbone, so the thought of something happening to him was more than she could stand. In fact she was directly in the room underneath his on the second floor.

When she was cleared, she immediately went upstairs to see him. And when she saw her baby daddy hooked up to all those machines, and his face madd swollen, she almost had a nervous breakdown. She had to be readmitted for close observation because her stress levels were off the chart, and the Doctors were afraid that she was on the verge of losing her baby by miscarriage. So, they sedated her, giving her meds to calm her nerves, and put her to sleep.

Harlem was walking down the Boulevard, and had stopped at Mc-Donalds, which was about a mile from the Hospital, to grab some grub when he got a call from one of the homeys that ColdWorld had breathed his last. He felt like he had just been hit with a ton of bricks. He screamed up to the sky, "Why, my nigga?!" he questioned as fat ass tears fell out of his eyes.

When he reached the hospital, he found everyone looking stunned, angry, and madd sad, and the hospital security straight clocking the situation, trying to keep shit under control. Cake was crying uncontrollably, and hugging a delirious Ms. Rosado tight. Serious was there holding it down for niggas, and being glue, trying to keep everybody together, and leading in prayer, asking God to give everybody strength, and to increase the peace in the streets, and cease the violence that is destroying young lives and tearing at the very fabric of the hood.

Serious was a real ass nigga, and got crazy humble when he got out of prison. He came back to the hood, and stood as a power of example for the homies. He was one of the original members of the North Common Fives, and was down when he was twelve.

He was one quick tempered dude that put in crazy work for the "Fives", and was on the frontline in all major beefs. But after, going to prison for his involvement in a gang shooting that went down at the park where all the niggas hang at the Bishop Markham Projects. While in Walpole he met an OG named Infamous from out of the Bronx who was an ex hitman for one of the most notorious drug cartels in New York. Infamous was serving forever and a day for twenty-eight bodies. Rumors were if they got him for every person he merked the numbers of bodies would be up in the seventies. Infamous became a Born Again Christian, and was well known and well respected by prisoners and guards alike. He always tried to break off a piece of knowledge to all the little niggas that came through the prison doors. He and Serious met in the weight room, and became cool, after which he invited Serious to the prison chapel to hear his and other old timers' testimonies. Most of who had been locked down twenty-five years or more straight. After hearing his testimony and studying the Bible with the brothers there, he became a Christian, giving his life to God.

He left prison a totally different man. He gave up selling drugs, and even dropped his set. Niggas was shocked that he stopped reppin "Five", especially when he was one of the niggas that started the team. But behind prison walls, he peeped the reality of what banging and selling drugs was doing to his hood and homies, and vowed to be a part of the solution instead of the problem. Serious saw so many young kats like him living behind prison walls, and who were never getting out, and he recognized it could've easily been him. He made a decision not to live that way anymore. While on lock, he used the resources that was available, and became determined to make something of himself.

When he got out, he used the loot he made at pre-release, and bought two old, but in fair condition vans, and started a Transportation Business. He was also doing volunteer work with "Coalition for a Better Acre", and working hard with his Church's Street Safe Anti-

Gang Initiative, trying to provide alternatives for niggas, who was out there caught up in banging and slanging. He worked hard to help his neighborhood to be a much safer place to live. He wasn't shy about telling anyone and everyone that it was the Power of God that changed his thuggish ways.

Mingo and a few of the other homies called him a sell-out for dropping his set, and had no love for him when he came through on his preaching shit. But he still lived in the hood, and regularly kicked it with the homies when he had time. He just didn't get down in any of their negativity. In fact, when he came to the block, he would always try to share his faith and love for God with the homies, telling them how such a dead end life slanging and banging was. He said that they needed to get God in their lives because He was the answer. Mingo would always come at him sideways telling him to stop trying to push a white man's God on niggas, cause they wasn't feeling it. ❏

CHAPTER ELEVEN

THE CRIB WAS CRAZY HUGE sitting up on the top of Andover Street. Out in front of the four car garage were three cars: two Range Rovers, one white and one black, and a black Mercedes Benz. It was obvious that this house was owned by someone with a real heavy cash flow, because only those with fat pockets could afford to live in a crib that big and that Fly. This section of Lowell had some of the dopest cribs, and was totally populated with those who were running the city, or the few who had hustled their way into crazy loot through a number of get money schemes. The Chief had purchased this house about a year and a half ago; he had brought a winning lottery ticket worth a million from a friend who owned a car dealership out on Drum Hill; rumors were he had strong armed the man into selling him the ticket for $300,000 cash. Truth was, he had beaten the man in a few high stakes golf games that he and some of the powers that be had going on for some years now, and the man ended up owing him $275,000. They worked it out, and the Chief ended up with the ticket.

"What the hell do you mean I'm not spending enough time home anymore?" Chief Ryan said perplexed.

"Remember the talk we had when you were considering that position? Let me refresh your memory. You told me when you became Chief it would provide you with more quality time for family things, and time for us to enjoy our lives," stated a thick white woman with sandy colored hair, pale skin and a diamond that looked about the size of a marble sitting on her left ring finger.

"Time, Karen. Have you watched the news lately or read the Lowell Sun? Hello, Earth to Karen. You must not be aware of what's going on in this city. There's gang wars, and kids dying from drug overdoses, not to mention citizens complaining to the Mayor about everything, and guess who's responsible for making these streets safe for ordinary citizens to walk without being shot or carjacked? Me, Karen, that's who. You know, the turn out for the last Folk Festival was the worst in its history with people saying they are not coming out because they didn't feel safe."

"There's a whole force down there. Why do you have to take on everything and play Superman? Family should be your main priority. We lost Jr. and now our Meagan is battling an addiction. Don't you think she deserves your time and attention? She needs her father. But you running around, trying to save other kids, when it's your own kid that needs you," she said angrily with tears forming in her eyes.

"What do you want from me, Karen? Look around you. I've given you everything. Trips, cars, jewelry, and one of the biggest homes on this friggin' street! How could you be unhappy or complaining, when any woman would be happy and feel like a queen?" Chief said pausing the TV where he had been watching Donald Trump talking about deporting illegal immigrants.

"What good is all this stuff if you're never around for us to enjoy it? You get up in the middle of the night and leave. And some nights you don't even come home, saying you're at the station, or out in the streets working on an investigation. Can't someone else do it? What are they down at the station, incompetent or something?" she said getting out of the La-Z-Boy seat to go get a Kleenex.

"I can't believe how ungrateful you are! I bust my ass trying to give you a life that I promised you and your parents I would give you, and now you act like it's not good enough." He responded scratching his head.

"What is it, John? You seeing another woman?" she said standing in front of him looking him straight in the eye.

"Another woman! You have to be kidding me, Karen," he answered with a big laugh.

"Do you see me laughing, John? Everything with you lately has been secretive. All these late-night meetings. And my gut keeps telling me you're up to no good. So for the sake of embarrassing me I would like to know who she is before I hear it from somewhere else, like the Lowell Sun. You used to tell me everything, including when you had to take a dump. Now you don't tell me nothing. We actually hardly talk anymore. I just don't understand what happened to us," she said sitting back in the La-Z-Boy wiping the tears.

"We have gotten rich that's what's happening, and it seems the more I do the more you complain. I don't know what the hell your problem is."

"Money, money, money. That's all you think of," she said blowing her nose.

"Mom, Dad," Meagan, their 19 year old daughter, came into the room."Why you guys always arguing lately? You never used to argue."

Meagan had been clean ever since she graduated from the Lowell House Program on Appleton Street where she was placed after her parents sectioned her. Her parents would spend many nights during her using days on the dark and cold streets looking for her, wondering if she was dead or in trouble, especially with the deadly heroin now on the streets

The dealers, in order to increase their profits, had been mixing heroin with fentanyl, and it was pushing addicts to the grave quick.

"We are fine, honey," Ms. Ryan said lying, not wanting to worry her daughter.

"Yeah, we are good. Just trying to work a few things out. How was your meeting honey?" Chief asked getting up, and reaching for his wallet to give his daughter some money for the mall.

"It went okay I spoke tonight. It was real scary to tell what happened, and what I did for drugs in front of all those people. But I managed, and actually felt better afterwards. I get my one year coin in a few months, and I want you guys to be there. How about a group hug before I go? Christina, my sponsor, will be here in ten minutes to pick me up," Meagan said spreading her arms out wide.

"What mall you going to?" Ms. Ryan asked getting up to hug her daughter and husband.

"Pheasant Lane. Come on, group hug!" Meagan answered squeezing her mom and dad. ❏

CHAPTER TWELVE

AFTER HARLEM LEFT THE HOSPITAL, he went home, and chilled in his room, looking at photos and videos of him and ColdWorld, reminiscing about his boy, and how fucked up shit was about to be. He spent his time chillin' in his room, listening to beats, and just writing lyrics about what went down which was something he did regularly to keep the stress off his chest. Harlem was crazy depressed, and had spent the past two days in his room not answering his phone, telling his mom to say he was sleeping if any one came knocking for him. He made a call to a florist on Merrimack Street, and ordered a custom arrangement for ColdWorld's Funeral. He wasn't sure what to wear to the wake or the funeral, and went to Mr. Tux's to get a hook up. After two days, the day of the wake, he began cleaning his room, and getting his shit together. He found a crack stem inside the pocket of his UMass Lowell hoody sweatshirt, and got heated waiting for his mom to come home to confront her about it. Things had been good as far as he could see with his mom. She had a new dude in her life. Harlem didn't care for him much, but if his mom was happy and staying clean, then it was peace with him.

"What's this?" Harlem asked his mom as soon as she walked in the door from work.

"Looks like a crack stem to me" she answered kicking off her shoes, and trying to get to the bathroom to pee.

"I know what it is! Tell me, why did I find it in the pocket of my hoody?" he asked aggressively like he knew she was caught.

"I don't have a clue! I don't fuck with that shit anymore, so I have no use for it. Now get out of my way. I got to go to the bathroom."

"I hope you ain't, cause that would be a mighty fucked up move.

But it was in the hoody you always use when it's a bit chilly out."

"I told you, it's not mine, and I didn't put it there. Maybe one of them trick ass girls you be messing with and bringing up in here put it in there," she said sarcastically.

"I doubt that cause I don't mess with bitches that are crackheads."

"Well, it could have been left there from when I was using. Who knows?" she responded from the bathroom.

"Yeah, whatever. Just hope you ain't fucking with that shit. You've been doing good and I'm proud of you."

"Thanks. That felt good hearing you say that. Honey, did Shelton come by here today?" she asked, changing the subject.

"Nah, I ain't seen dude. I know you ain't getting serious with that dude. You just met him a couple months ago, Ma," he said looking at her.

"That's none of your business how serious we are. You seem like you got something against him."

"Nah, actually I don't. But just want you to make sure he real, cause a lot of them kats be on some playing a chick shit, and only want one thing."

"Well, don't worry. I ain't that stupid. At least that much I know. Shit, I've been around nothing but players, and ain't got played yet. If anything, I'm the one doing the playing!" she said proudly putting her hands on her hips. "How's things with Ms. Rosado? And when is the wake and funeral?"

"I haven't really spoken to anyone, so I don't know. But the wakes today, and the funeral is on Saturday."

"Your friend Serious keeps coming by asking for you. Said he's been calling your phone, but no answer."

"Yeah, I know. I just needed time to get with myself, and mourn my nigga my way, you know?"

"What I tell you about using that word in my house? Oh, you got this letter from the DMV," she said handing him a white envelope.

Harlem opened the letter, and a smile came on his face. It was a letter granting him back his license upon the payment of $250. "Yo! You know what this means? I'm about to get a whip!" he yelled waving the letter in the air, and dancing the Shmoney dance.

"Yeah, it's about time. Well, I gotta get in the shower, and get out of here. Shelton's taking me out to a nice, fine restaurant," she said licking her big lips.

"Yeah, whatever. Acting like you ain't never been on a date before."

Harlem went out into the hallway, and threw the stem into the incinerator, again opening up the letter and re-reading it. It'd been three years since he got stopped on Market Street, and his license was revoked. He was found guilty of possession of crack with the intent to distribute. Harlem had saved up his dough, and had enough to get that black-on-black Honda Civic that Serious was selling, plus still re-up on a package. Something inside of him told him his mom was fucking up, but he didn't see any obvious signs, so he didn't stress it. He went back into his room, and checked his stash spot. Shit was still good. His money and drugs were still in their hiding spot, untouched.

When his mom came out of the bathroom he jumped in the shower, got dressed, and headed out to meet up with his homies. They all were about to crack a bottle of Henny, which was ColdWorld's favorite drink, and the way niggas saluted their bro. After getting a little drizzy, he had to get up with his girl, Lauren, and break out to ColdWorld's wake.

ColdWorld's wake was crazy packed. It seemed like the whole projects came through to show the proper love and respect to the homey. ColdWorld was dressed up in a light blue suit, the color that represented the North Common Fives, with matching Jordans 1's. In fact, the whole team wore the same Jordans, even though they all had on tuxes.

Harlem received a text while inside the funeral home. It was from Toy, she put him hip to a dope fiend named Lies that had heard who shot ColdWorld, and that it was a dude named Chopper, who was kicking it with a girl named Leah that worked with Lauren at the Burlington Coat Factory in Billerica. The fiend went with Leah's dope fiend aunt, and had heard Chopper on the phone one day talking to another nigga about it.

Harlem pulled Mingo and a few other homies outside the funeral home and showed them the text.

"Yo, we gotta find this nigga ASAP, and I'm gonna empty my shit out in him. When I'm done with this nigga he gonna look like a piece of Swiss cheese. Facts," Mingo said.

"No doubt. But first we gotta find out where the nigga rest. I'm gonna holla at Lauren to try to find out more about this chick Leah," Harlem said.

"For sure, my nigga. I told you it wouldn't be long before we get at the nigga who did this," Kizz said smiling.

"You're right, there's no silence in the streets. Shit always comes to the surface out here. Yo dawg, I know somebody knows where this kat or what set he from," Mingo said still clocking the text.

"Should be easy to find. Toy said she ran into the fiend who told her he had some important info he would give her for some brown. He was madd dope sick at the time. So she hit him with a couple of dollars, and he straight spilled his guts. After we bounce from here we will go get up with Toy. She should be off work by then. She would have been here, but her boss would've fired her ass if she took the day off, telling her she had a choice of going to the wake or the funeral. So she chose to pull show at the funeral."

"Yo, let's get back in there. This is madd disrespectful to our nigga," Kizz said opening the door to the funeral parlor.

Mingo shot Kizz a crazy look, and then they all followed Harlem back into the Wake.

"Man, that nigga gets on my last nerve. He always got something stupid to say," Mingo whispered to Harlem.

"Just chill, my nigga, for real chill. You know Mrs. Rosado don't want you here in the first place. I spoke with her to make it cool for you be here. I told her you and Serious were the ones that raised all the bread for the funeral and shit, so she letting you slide on that strength," Harlem said. ❏

CHAPTER THIRTEEN

AFTER COLDWORLD'S MURDER, the police stepped up their presence preparing for a retaliation shooting or gang war. They knew when shit like this happened, niggas acted up. They weren't sure what crews were involved, so they posted up on all four major communities where the major gangs reside. The Sheriff's Department's big ass Mobil Command Center was set up in the North Common Projects' parking lot by the swimming pool. It was the latest crime fighting tool, which had on board the latest high-tech electronic and technology equipment. The fucked up thing was they purchased it with forfeited drug funds that they took off of niggas. The shit was so bananas that its camera and surveillance system could hear and peep a conversation, or read a license plate, from three blocks away. It was capable of identifying a face from the same distance. They had planned to keep a tight surveillance. The gang task force went hard, going from door to door in the projects, passing out anti-violence fliers, and asking residents if they had seen or heard anything. The FBI and DEA also had been called in to assist the gang task force.

The day of the funeral it was drizzling out, but warm. Harlem was asked by Ms. Rosado to be a pallbearer, along with a few of ColdWorld's family members and cousins. This was the eleventh funeral he attended so far this year. It was hard for Harlem to believe or accept his day-one-nigga, ColdWorld, being dealt this bad hand.

But he understood that in this game, shit is always like that. You never know whose card would be pulled. The streets just had a fucked up way of choosing.

Harlem looked and saw the Chief of Police and the Mayor in the funeral audience, sitting up front in the second row behind Ms.

Rosado. There was also a couple of unmarked police cars parked outside across the street gathering intel by taking pictures of everybody. He and his team filled the last three rows on the left side.

After Ms. Rosado and family members said their peace, she called Serious to come up to the podium, calling him by his government Jonathan Bryar, to come forward, and say a few things.

"Yo this sell out ass nigga really think he something," Mingo said nudging Harlem.

"This ain't the time, my nigga. Fall back, for real," Harlem said without even looking at Mingo.

"Good afternoon family. It's a sad day when we come here to say goodbye, and pay our last respects to a brother who shouldn't be laying in a casket, but instead be in a classroom at UMass Lowell. But we live in a time where there is so much violence and hate that we in the hood are lucky if we live pass the age of eighteen. I know this room is filled with pain, anguish and heartbreak as it fills my thuggish heart also. In honor of my friend's life, I myself will use the memory of his life to fuel me daily as I fight to save the lives of young people, so that we will have less funerals, and more graduation ceremonies, and I invite you to join me in celebrating his life that way."

Serious ended to a standing applause. Everybody, but Mingo and a few others, were clapping. After the funeral, a long line of cars went up Gorham Street to the Edison Cemetery where the homey was laid to real rest.

Harlem and his friends headed back to the hood where a cookout was awaiting them, and they sat and ate, listening to some of Cold-World's favorite songs, and shared stories about him. When Toy showed up, she approached Harlem, and they went for a walk around the projects to kick it. She told him about the fiend, and then dialed a number he had given her, but no one answered. It went straight to voicemail.

Harlem was in a daze, and busy looking at a bunch of neighborhood kids who were preoccupied with flies buzzing around a dead rat near a garbage can.

"Yo, the nigga didn't answer. Don't know if the number is real or fake," she said following Harlem's eyes to the dead rat.

"That's okay. I'm going to holla at Lauren about the chick, Leah, at her job to see what she can find out for me," Harlem said.

"That's what's up, and I'll keep both my ears to the street. Trust me, we're gonna find dude."

"Yeah I know that. If that's the last thing that I ever do," Harlem said hugging Toy.

"Oh, you owe me $200, homie," she said sticking her hand out.

"What I owe you for? You bugging right now?"

"Nah I ain't. That's what I gave to that fiend for the info. Shit, it was my car payment, and I couldn't get in touch with you, so I put it up," Toy said sincerely.

Harlem reached in his pocket, peeled off a few bills from his knot, and hit her with the loot. He knew nothing was free when it came to Toy. She didn't give a fuck who it was, she stayed on her bread game.

❏

CHAPTER FOURTEEN

THE FIRST LARGE SHIPMENT OF DRUGS had arrived and was ready to be picked up. Bonz and his homie, Nick, went to meet up with the son of the Funeral Home Director on the Boulevard, and picked up a duffle bag full of China White Heroin and Fish Scale Cocaine. There were also 10,000 Perc 30 pills in the bag. They had already met with Harlem and the other gang heads, and kicked it about what was going down, and how each set would get only what they could handle.

Bonz had stressed that the best way to distribute the drugs was to leave it in its purest form, but didn't really give a fuck what or how they did it as long as when his man came through to pick up the loot, there was definitely no shorts. He had planned to meet up with Harlem personally, and hit him with the bulk of the drugs, and most of the Percs for a connect Harlem had that owned a Strip Club up in Worcester called Hurricane Betty's. Shit, he was paying top dollar for them shits, so Harlem would be making double on what he got them for. They drove to Walker Street to a house full of little niggas that they used to take full inventory of the drugs, weighing it and separating it into packages and putting codes on them to be delivered to the sets.

The next morning Nick brought what was remaining, which was about four keys of cocaine and sixteen bricks of heroin, to City Hall where he worked as a janitor, and stashed it there. It was a madd cool spot for a stash, and only Nick knew of it, and only he would have complete access to it. He had created the illest hiding place inside a wall in the basement, right up under the noses of those in power. It was crazy, yet ingenious. After all, no one would expect City Hall to be the stash house for the biggest drug operation in the city.

The new drug was madd potent and had fiends turnt all the way up, and chasing hard. Motherfuckers were coming as far away as Maine to cop the shit. It even raised the crime levels as fiends were hustling harder, robbing and stealing, and doing whatever to get another blast. All the sets were getting money, and eating off of bigger plates. And it showed because they were flossing their new found wealth: buying up dope ass whips, flashy jewelry and shutting down the mall buying bags of top of the line gear. And everybody took notice. Even the Lowell Police who began collaborating with the Feds and DEA, trying to find out where all the drugs, new money, and out-of-town traffic had come from, not to mention the drastic increase of crime in the City.

They hit the streets hard, kicking in doors and snatching up the prostitutes, fiends and little niggas out their trapping on corners trying to find someone to break and tell them what the fuck was going on and who was the top dog on this New Jack City type movement. They knew that whoever it was, they had a serious connect because it seemed like in a matter of a few weeks the whole city had become one giant drug store.

Harlem and his niggas was killing it, making $30,000 - $40,000 a day, and eating very well. Harlem stayed in the studio working, and turning up on his music. He was the Tom Brady of the "Fives", so he just quarterbacked, and called the plays, making sure everybody was moving their work and playing their own positions. He used Mingo to play everything close he was in charge of picking up and counting the money along with Lauren and Toy.

His crazy ass blood thirsty nigga Lethal who had just came home from upstate was the muscle keeping all things correct and making sure no one stepped out of line, if they did he corrected it by force.

No questions asked and no one exempt. Any nigga that fucked up was eligible to get dealt with.

Harlem had met up with a producer that had caught a whiff of his mixtape "Lowell's Finest" on the internet and off of the Launch Pad, and hit him up asking him to come to Boston for a sit down. Harlem met with Producer Kane1 in a studio in the basement of a beauty salon in the Grove Hall section of Roxbury. At their first meeting he told Harlem about his own past and how he repped a set at one time, and that he got locked up for killing his cousin who repped a different block two streets over from his set. He took his case to the hoop and only by the Mercy of Allah he beat it on a technicality. Being caught up like that not knowing if you're ever gonna come home opened his third eye and when he came home he was on some new and improved shit, putting his gun and drug game to sleep.

He told Harlem that he had a real gift in him and in order for Harlem to make it he would have to work crazy hard, stay focused and leave the banging and drug game alone, because it is a known killer of talent. He had seen many with crazy talent, destroy themselves by being caught up in the streets trying to be Billy Bad Ass. He also let him know he had no time for a nigga that played a dead man's game, and he would not associate with anyone no matter how much talent they had, who couldn't make a smart decision of life over death. For he wasn't down with signing a nigga who could be a liability to his own plans and dreams because of his affiliation and drug selling. He told Harlem to really search himself and find out if it's something he wanted to do. If so he would rock with him.

The money was coming in loads and Harlem was stacking more bread than ever and couldn't see himself leaving the game or his niggas behind or fading to black on them. So he kept Kane1 on pause on the back burner telling him he'd get back to him as soon as he made a decision and he just kept trapping and hitting the studio on his own figuring he would make it happen his way.

They had got word and found out who the nigger Chopper was and where he laid his head. The word was that he was living on the Southside on Kinsman Street by Frank & Ernie's with his girl Leah and her aunt. They had found out that the nigger Chopper was trying to get down with the Southside, so they told him in order to get down he would have to prove himself and loyalty. They told him he had to go to one of the enemy hoods and spray it up. He chose Harlem's hood because that was the hood who had murked his little cousin, TwoShoes, who was killed in a beef with a "Five" named LastBreath, who stabbed him to death at the Black Festival at Shedd Park. Chopper was only eighteen and just had twins a boy and a girl who was six months old with Leah.

"Yo, we bout to ride out over to that nigga Chopper's crib and hit him up," Harlem said into the phone to Lethal.

"Come through and snatch me up dawg," said a sleepy rough voice

"Where you at?" Harlem asked between drags of the blunt of K2.

"I'm at the bat cave nigga, Mama's crib."

"Shit, nigga you act like I know where you are, shit since you been home you been all over the place diving in madd honeys," Harlem said laughing and choking on the smoke.

"Facts, shit, just making up for all the time I ain't seen no booty, ya feel me?" He said matter of fact.

"I got you dawg. Give me like twenty minutes. I'm still waiting for Mingo and Kizz to come through with the burners and hotbox."

"Cool, just hit me when you're on your way. I'm 'bout to roll up," Lethal said reaching for the backwoods and bag of weed off the end table.

"That's a fact, yo. How everything go last night?" he asked curiously.

"It was gravy. Niggas sold out. Missed out on crazy dough though.

Shit, fiends were still hitting up the Shmoney Jack all night, but niggas couldn't serve them because we couldn't get in touch with you for the re-up. So we just drank, smoked and shot dice. Yo, that nigga Kizz is one lucky motherfucker. He got us for about $1100. Shit, Mingo was 'bout to shoot the nigga thinking he was cheating. He got Mingo for his bracelet. I had to stop the nigga from pulling out on him with his drunk ass!"

"What? That nigga just got us last weekend for about $1600! Shit, that's that beginner's luck. Shit, cause he just started G'ing with us," Harlem said surprised.

"Yeah, it may be beginner's luck or either the nigga got the dice from the joke shop for real my nigga. Shit we gotta check that niggas dice, he may be doing some David Copperfield type shit on niggas, cause ain't that much fucking luck in the world."

"I feel you my nigga. If that nigga is pulling stunts, then you know that nigga is getting served and we are tossing his pockets until they resemble rabbit ears, and that's my word dawg."

"No bull, you know that's right. But you gotta get in line nigga cause I'm laying hands on him first for my little bit of bread. Plus the nigga got me when I was crazy fucked up on that Henny and Perc mix, that shit had my eyes crossed," Lethal said laughing.

"Yo, yo, yo, hold up my nigga. I thought we talked about that Perc and pill popping shit. You know that shit ain't cool. You already know how I feel about that. Shit, you keep playing with that stuff, and the next thing you know you'll be a fucking fiend lining up for that Brown," Harlem said seriously.

"Ahh, nigga you bugging right now. I will never be a fiend. It ain't in my blood. Actually it ain't no room cause all the blood in me is gangsta. Ya heard me? You talking madd reckless, my nigga." Lethal said getting a little tight.

"I'm dead ass, nigga. Just stop fucking with that shit. It's for suckers. Shit, just get your smoke and drink on that gets a nigga right enough. And I'm telling you not asking you."

"Oh so you pulling rank on me huh dawg?"

"That's a double fact. I have to my nigga who else is going to protect the team and what we doing if I don't? Shit, we got too much going on to be fucking with shit that twists a nigga's thinking. I need you 100% on point for real. Ain't no room for slipping or mistake making. A nigga gotta be on point extra, chasing this paper," Harlem said with authority.

"My nigga, you talking to a nigga that stays on point, and ain't no pill gonna knock me off my center. I'm built better than that. You know how we do."

"I know it ain't cause you ain't fucking with it no more. Yo this nigga Mingo is hitting me up. Be ready. I'll hit you when I'm on my way."

"Aiight one."

"One," Harlem said.

Mingo and Kizz picked Harlem up in front of Rancho Tipico on Salem Street in an older model Black Ford Explorer they had stolen out of Nashua, New Hampshire. When he got into the back seat, he saw a 40 Glock sitting on the floor, and grabbed it in his gloved hand. He was feeling good about the fact they were finally going to get this nigga. Then ColdWorld could rest in peace. He also wondered about the new beef it was going to start with them kats on the Southside. They had just recently called a truce with them on the strength of getting money. It was Bonz that brought them together. Actually, Harlem did time and had been in the same unit as the nigga Hardy, who was Haitian, and ran them Southside kats. But shit, there was no other way to dead the issue until this nigga Chopper was pushing up daisies. Whatever happened after, they would have to deal with any repercussions. They drove over to snatch up Lethal who came out fully fatigued up like he was 'bout to go fight Isis or something. The nigga was super crazy when it came to drama, and he went extra for the niggas he rocked with. Shit, at seven years old the nigga stabbed his baby sitter with a pen, just because she snatched the controller out of his hand.

Then in sixth grade he smacked his math teacher. He was always wildin', and he loved drama.

They were passing around a bottle of Henny on their way across town to the Southside, taking all the cuts to avoid being ran up on by Five-0. When they got to the address they rode past it, and went around the block again checking the scene before stopping on the side street that would lead them quickly back onto Thorndike Street and then 495 where they were going to go and get rid of the car on Tanner Street where there was nothing but used car lots and hood type car repair shops which the Explorer would blend in perfectly. From there Mingo's girl would pick them up and shoot them back to the Northside where they would take off all their clothes and put them in a giant garbage bag to be burnt in the incinerator.

They saw a light on in the green house on the second floor. No cars in the garage. Kizz was good at getting into cribs and brought his tools to key the door. They went to the side door through the garage and split up. The house was on the end of the street so a chance of a neighbor peeping them was madd slim. Mingo and Kizz took the upstairs and Harlem and Lethal downstairs. They heard music coming from the basement and crept down to check. Mingo entered a room upstairs to find a female laying down sleep in Victoria Secret pajamas. She seemed like she may be white or Puerto Rican. He noticed two children sleeping in two cribs against the wall, one dressed in pink and the other in blue. As he walked closer the floor made a creaking sound waking the girl on the bed. She turned wiping her eyes and found herself staring into the barrel of a gun before she was able to let out a scream.

"Where the fuck is your nigga, Chopper?" Mingo asked angrily through gritted teeth.

"He's not here I don't know where he is," she said shaking badly.

"Yo, bitch I'm serious! I know you know where and if you want to live to see those two little babies reach their first birthday, you better tell me!"

"I don't know! He left a couple hours ago with his boy Thrillz. Said they had shit to do," she said beginning to get scared, looking at her sleeping babies.

"Well, you better call the nigga and tell him you need him to come back to the crib cause one of the babies is sick and in trouble. And you better not try anything slick," Mingo said walking towards the crib with the Glock still pointed at the girl.

Mingo snatched up one of the babies by the leg, and opened up the bedroom window dangling the crying baby out the window and threatening to drop it if she wasn't successful in getting Chopper home. She grabbed her cell phone shaking so badly she could barely dial a number. Having to start dialing over trying to compose herself, while staring at her daughter Janeah crying and held upside down.

"Yo, what the fuck you doing dawg!" Harlem asked Mingo when he saw a little girl at the end of his arm upside down hanging out a window.

"Trying to get the job done. Shit I ain't got no mercy for nothing or no one in this house, and you shouldn't either. Our nigga is dead and there was no mercy extended to him so why you acting soft?"

"Nigga, put that baby back in that crib. We ain't no fucking savages," Harlem said pointing to the crib.

"Speak for yourself," he said putting the Glock in his waist and grabbing up the other baby with his free hand. "Now bitch, get that nigga here fast or they going and then I'ma bout to throw your ass out this window behind them!"

"I said put them back," Harlem said walking towards him.

"Stop my nigga! You come any closer and I will kill these non-flying mother fuckers."

At that Lethal and Kizz entered the room. They all had black bandanas and knitted black caps on making it hard to tell who they were. Lethal came in and saw the scene and began laughing madd hard.

"Yo, that's what's up my nigga! That will make the bitch get the nigga here ASAP!"

"For sure!" Kizz replied.

The girl received a text and read it aloud to them. It was from Chopper who said he was getting off the highway and would be there after he dropped Thrillz off. To give him about 10 minutes. Mingo put the crying kids on the bed with their mother.

"Now you have to shut those little mother fuckers up," he said keeping the gun pointed at her.

"Yo, we will talk about this shit later," Harlem said madd disturbed.

"Nothing to talk about Fam, I came to do a job and like you said nothing or none gets in the way of getting at the nigga, and in my eyes that includes you."

Harlem looked at Mingo really wanting to take his head off, but for some reason respected him for going hard.

"Yo Lethal, you and Kizz go hide in the garage and meet the nigga when he come through the door, and bring him up here."

"Cool, come on Kizz. Time to put in that wizzork, baby," Lethal said heading out of the bedroom.

"Mingo put them in the closet," Harlem said going to the window to look out, and then closed it.

"Please, I promise not to start any trouble, just let me and my babies stay right here please!" the girl begged.

Harlem looked at Mingo who shrugged his shoulder as if it was his call.

"Listen we are not going to hurt you or the babies, we are only here for Chopper, I have no interest in you or them," Harlem said pointing to the babies who had fell back to sleep after given their pacifiers.

"Thank you," the girl said still visibly shaking.

"Yo, Harlem." ❑

CHAPTER FIFTEEN

F.B.I. SPECIAL AGENT IN CHARGE BRUCE BLACKWELL paced up and down the room filled with law enforcement representing different levels and agencies. He had called this meeting after receiving an anonymous tip in regards to an organized drug dealing operation involving the local gangs and even some City Officials who were collaborating together and responsible for the large amounts of heroin, cocaine and almost any other drug in popular demand on the streets of Lowell.

"Gentlemen, I thank you for being here and arriving on time," he said over chuckles and laughter from the men in the room. We are all well aware of the increase of drug flow in the city, and the District Attorney is breathing down our necks wondering what we are doing about it. The other day I and the head of the Lowell Drug Task Force had a rather lengthy conversation with the Mayor in regards to the major increase in crime and violence. We are also aware that it is and always is drugs that bring heavy increases. We also know from a CI that the local street gangs, especially the North Common Fives are moving great amounts of these drugs and so is the Belvidere 460's. We've also got intel there are city officials involved and playing the major roles. We don't know who these people are or what level in local government they are in. We do know that we are assigned to dismantle this organization. Captain Russell from the Lowell Gang Unit will be responsible for drawing information from contacts who will provide us with information on each gang and the part they are playing. I want to know everything about each gang including where they sleep, shit and at what time. Understood?

Deputy Mitchell from The Middlesex Sheriff's Department will be responsible for intel from the inside, and extracting information from prisoners housed in his facility. There's a lot of potential information there if we could get those guys in there to talk.

On our team we will also have the DEA and Drug Task Force as well as other Agencies. We will meet again same time same place next week. Unless we have already eradicated these scum who are pushing drugs and violence. Anyone who gets even an iota of information pass it on to your commanding officer. Please do not overlook anything or anyone, everyone out there could be the one to provide the right info to lead us to the top who are calling the shots. So pay close attention especially to the junkies, crackheads and prostitutes who love talking with us," he finished with a smile. ❏

A THOUSAND THUGS

Darryl's mother, Mrs. Louella Richardson Buchannan, to whom he dedicated the book, and recognizes is the reason for his success. She said he could be anything. He finally believed her.

DARRYL E. BUCHANNAN

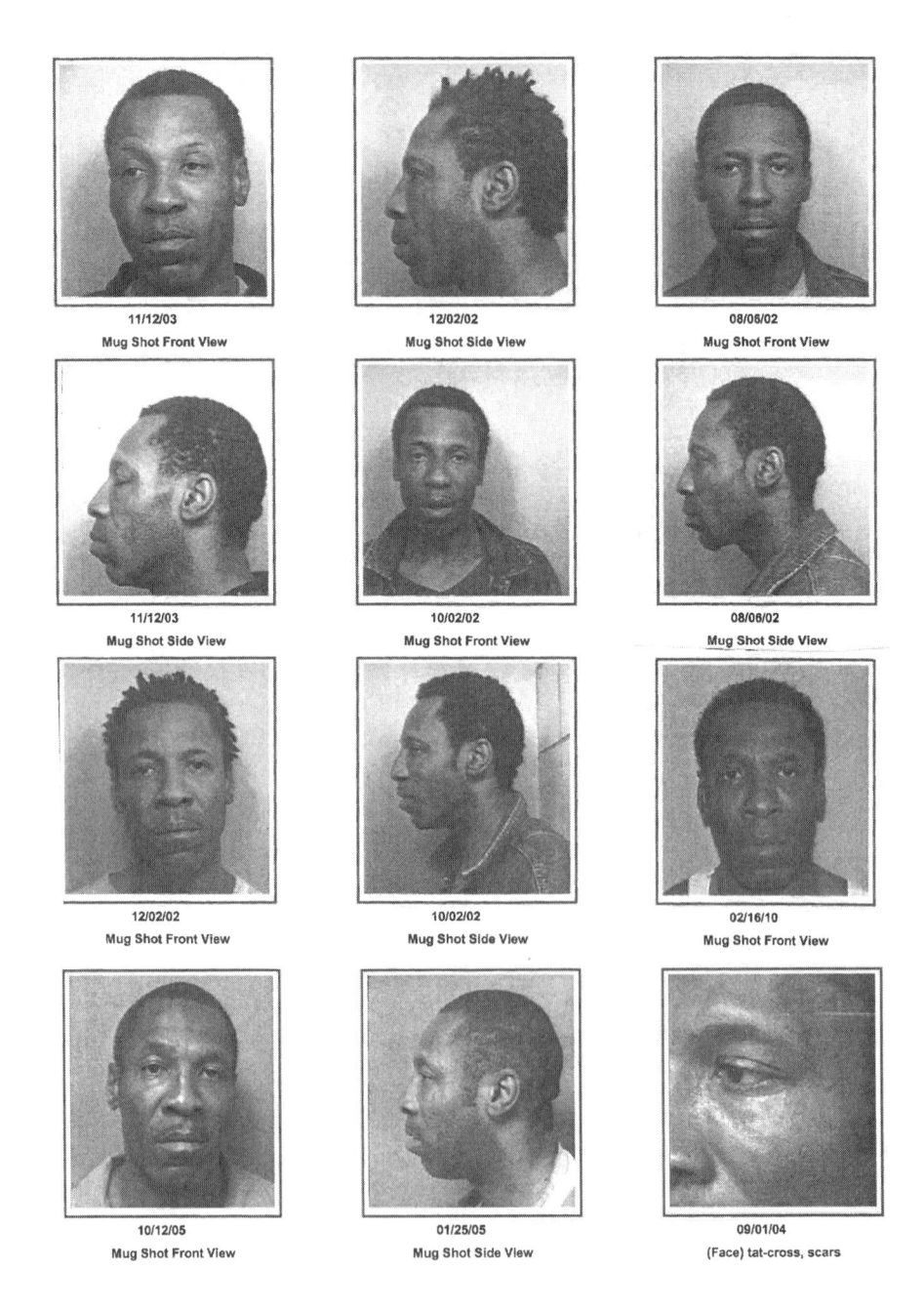

11/12/03 Mug Shot Front View	12/02/02 Mug Shot Side View	08/08/02 Mug Shot Front View
11/12/03 Mug Shot Side View	10/02/02 Mug Shot Front View	08/08/02 Mug Shot Side View
12/02/02 Mug Shot Front View	10/02/02 Mug Shot Side View	02/16/10 Mug Shot Front View
10/12/05 Mug Shot Front View	01/25/05 Mug Shot Side View	09/01/04 (Face) tat-cross, scars

Booking photos of Darryl throughout his 28 years of incarceration.

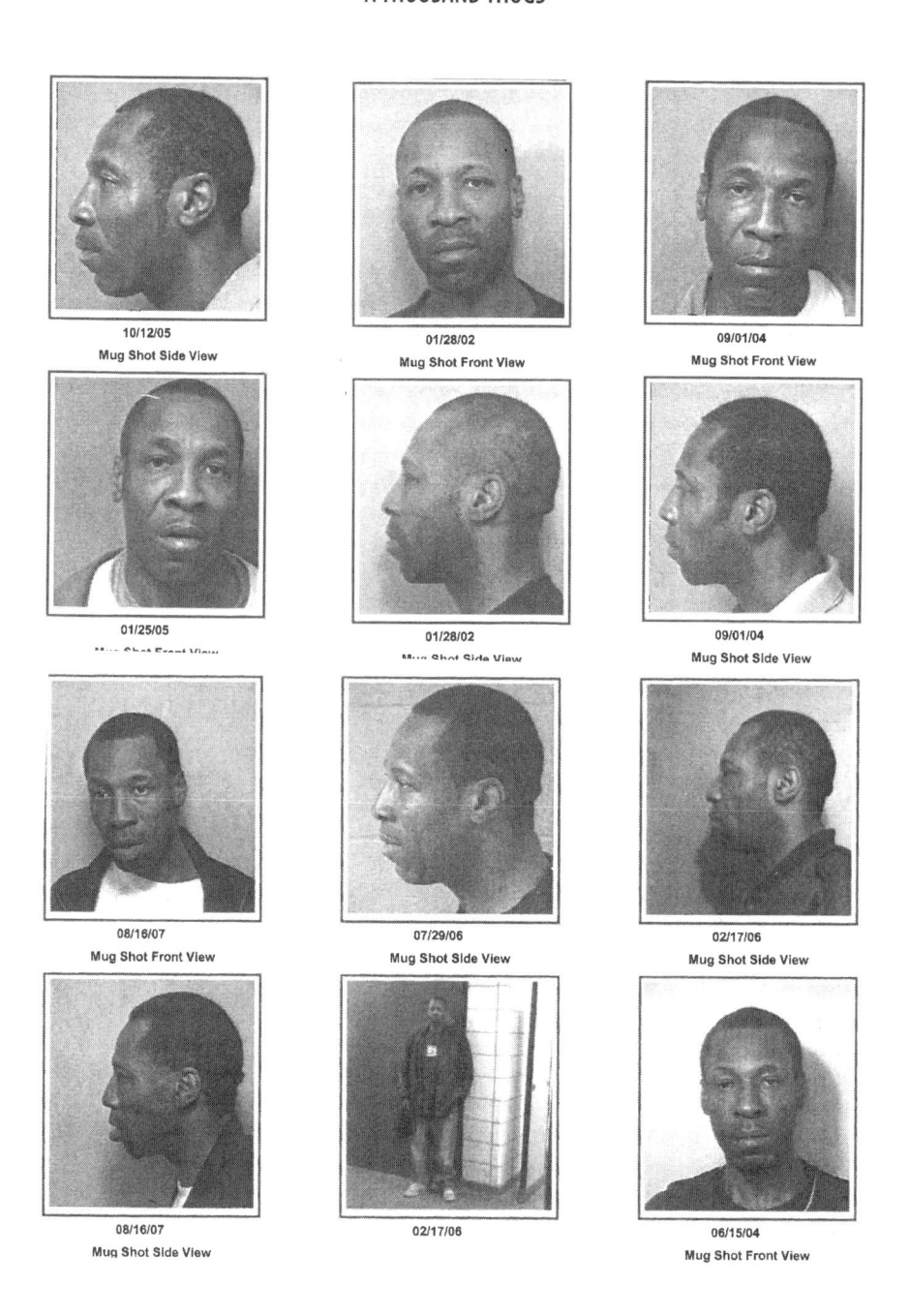

A THOUSAND THUGS

Booking photos of Darryl throughout his 28 years of incarceration.

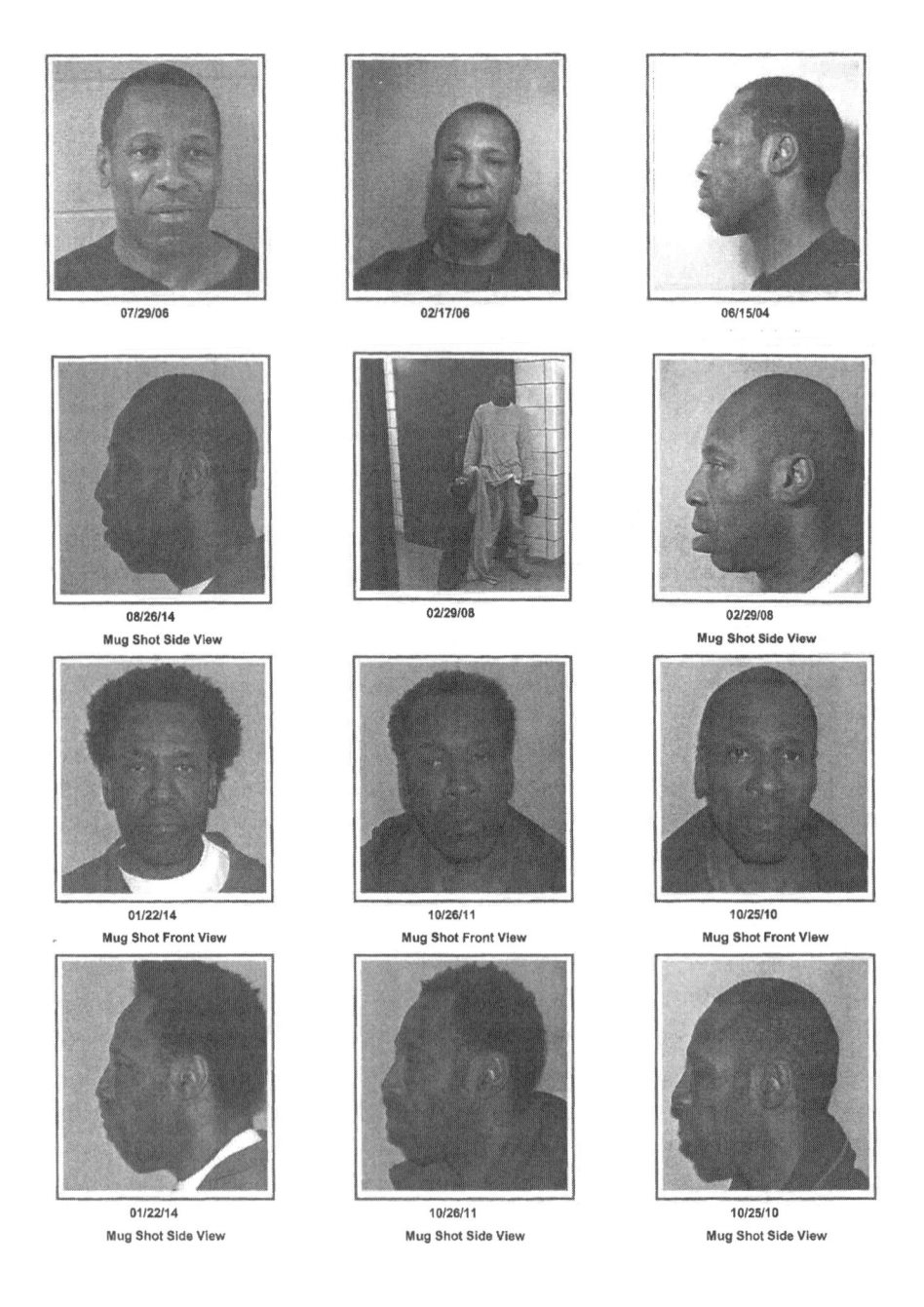

DARRYL E. BUCHANNAN

07/29/06

02/17/06

06/15/04

08/26/14
Mug Shot Side View

02/29/08

02/29/08
Mug Shot Side View

01/22/14
Mug Shot Front View

10/26/11
Mug Shot Front View

10/25/10
Mug Shot Front View

01/22/14
Mug Shot Side View

10/26/11
Mug Shot Side View

10/25/10
Mug Shot Side View

Booking photos of Darryl throughout his 28 years of incarceration.

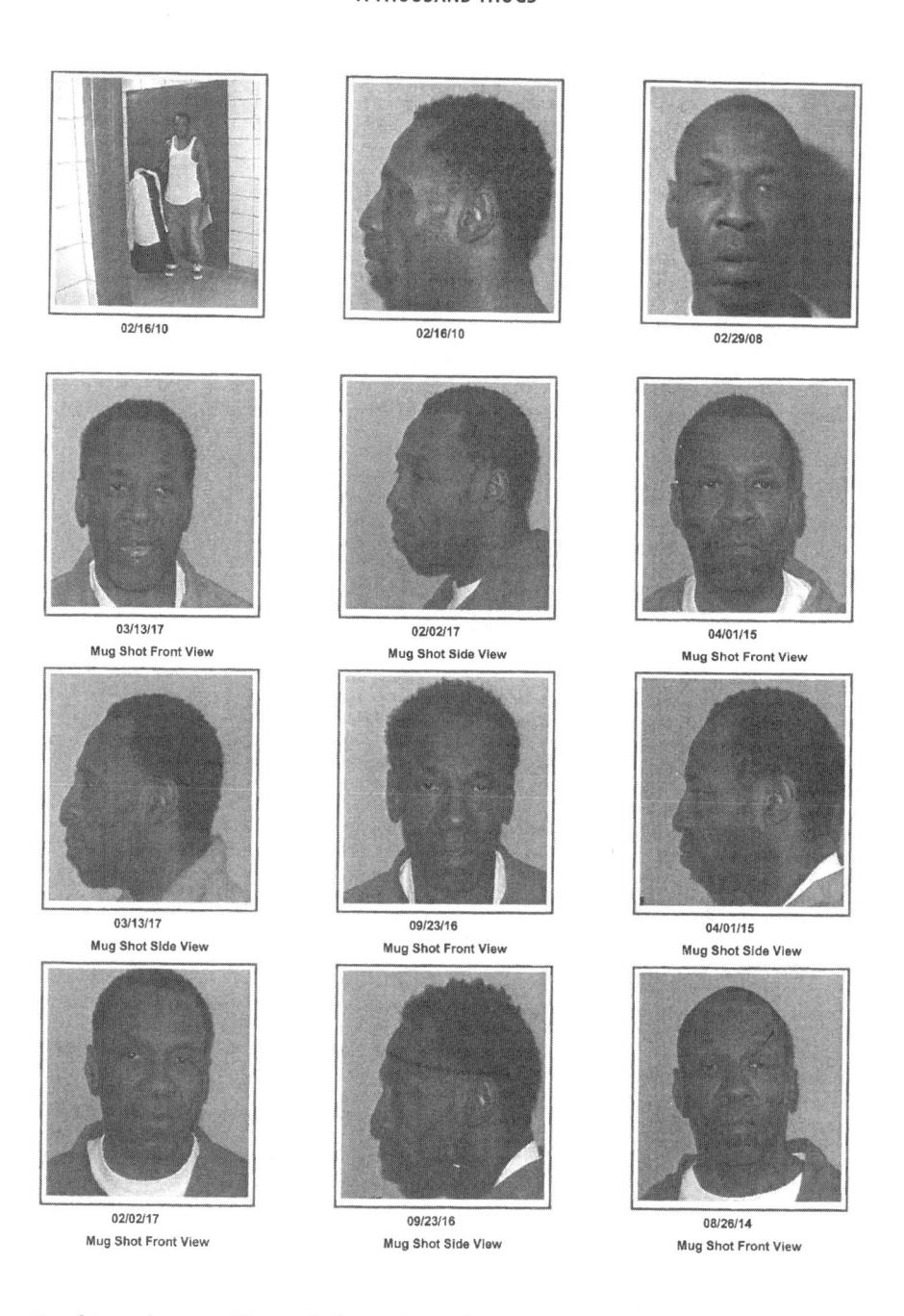

A THOUSAND THUGS

02/16/10

02/16/10

02/29/08

03/13/17
Mug Shot Front View

02/02/17
Mug Shot Side View

04/01/15
Mug Shot Front View

03/13/17
Mug Shot Side View

09/23/16
Mug Shot Front View

04/01/15
Mug Shot Side View

02/02/17
Mug Shot Front View

09/23/16
Mug Shot Side View

08/26/14
Mug Shot Front View

Booking photos of Darryl throughout his 28 years of incarceration.

DARRYL E. BUCHANNAN

The dream fulfilled. I'm picking up my published books today!

Darryl signing books in his hood, North Common Projects, Lowell, MA

A THOUSAND THUGS

Darryl standing on the steps of Lowell City Hall with his boyhood dream in his hand, "A Thousand Thugs".

DARRYL E. BUCHANNAN

Darryl and Robin Brown sharing a moment at the Book Signing Picnic at North Common Projects.

Darryl and his sister Maria. Her smile says it all. Proud of her brother.

A THOUSAND THUGS

Darryl and Officer Kevin posted up for a pic at the Lowell House. "I remember when they use to put cuffs on me, now they taking photos with me. What is in this cop's hand? Not a warrant, but my book "A Thousand Thugs". Yeah life is climbing."

Carolyn Ruf, Editor of "A Thousand Thugs" and Co-Founder of B.A.B.N.A.B., with Middlesex County District Attorney Marion Ryan, and Director of Community Partnership, Shawn MacMaster. D.A. Ryan has her own copy of "A Thousand Thugs".

Darryl and Louie posted up at the Book Release Picnic at North Common, Lowell

Darryl and Louie chillin in front of Darryl's ride, one of the gifts of sobriety.

Darryl at Danvers Detox where he was invited to give his message of hope.

Darryl and Frank at the Peer Recovery in Lawrence, MA. Frank, an ex-Lawrence Probation Officer, is now working in the Recovery Field. 2017

A THOUSAND THUGS

Darryl and Doug at Lawrence Peer Recovery where Darryl gave a message and began a Book Club. 2017

Darryl's 2 heartbeats: his daughter Tyrisha and grandson Jayden. Jayden is the logo for BABNAB. North Common Block Picnic & Book Signing, Lowell.

Darryl and Katy siging books at "Everyday Miracles Peer Recovery Center" Book Club in Worcester after his presentation.

Darryl speaking at Recovery Connection Picnic in Marlborough. Recovery Month September 2017.

Darryl and his fiancée, Katy. New Beginnings.

Lowell Boys & Girls Club.

Darryl and Sully from the Rock Band "Godsmack" posted up for a photo. Sully said This book's for me. Darryl smiled and said, "For Sure."

A THOUSAND THUGS

Darryl and his cousin Anthony in Boston, MA.

Darryl and Robin Brown at an Opioid Awareness Event in Waltham, MA.

Darryl & Will posted up in front of the Lowell House where he was asked to speak at the Matador Program. Thanks Deptuty Lewis.

DARRYL E. BUCHANNAN

Darryl and his confidant Brandon at the Marlborough Drug Awareness Event.

Darryl posted up in front of his building at North Common Projects. He use to smoke crack and sleep on the stairs while caught in his addiction.

A THOUSAND THUGS

Darryl posted up with the One organization at the Andover Cares Event.

Darryl & his childhood homey Carlos.

Darryl & his daughter Ty in Dorchester, MA.

DARRYL E. BUCHANNAN

CHAPTER SIXTEEN

HARLEM LEFT THE DENTIST OFFICE in his Range Rover that he bought from a used car dealer, and headed back to the Acre to meet up with Bonz at his crib. He hated being late, but for some reason his time management was always fucked up. Bonz had said it was important that they build asap. Last night he didn't get too much sleep. He was tossing and turning all night. Lauren had broken the news to him over dinner at the Mill City Barbeque & Grill that she was pregnant, and he was about to be a daddy. He had crazy mixed feelings about it. Things have been going great, money was good and after killing Chopper the team got back to getting money. Shit, at one time the police had flooded sets and arresting niggas on petty charges and bringing them down to the station questioning them all about Chopper's murder. Shit, the case probably got more priority because of what bugged out ass Mingo did with the babies, cause Lord knows it was nothing to kill a hood nigger it didn't even register on the catch them scale. But to fuck with babies and woman, was a definite no-no.

"Is Bonz there?" He said to a pretty Asian girl with an angelic face and jet black hair that answered the door. Harlem wondered if she was Bonz's girl. If it was, the nigga was madd lucky cause she was fly as all hell. She had eyes like a doe and a nice slim body and a perfect round butt, and her tight jeans gave her booty a voice that spoke to his zipper.

"No, he's not here. He had an appointment in Lawrence," she said staring in Harlem's face as if she was about to eat him.

"Damn yo, I was supposed to meet him here can you try hitting him up?"

"Yes no problem," she said softly, turning and leaving the door open and Harlem's eyes feasted and followed her small round booty.

"No, he's not answering, but you can come inside and wait if you like. He should be here if he said he would," she said leading him into the living room that had a big ass flat screen that was as big as the wall.

"Facts, I'll parlay for a few, see if he shows," Harlem said copping a squat on the thick sofa.

"So, you from around here? I never seen you before," she asked curiously.

"Yeah that's a fact. I grew up here in the Acre, in the building right across from the school."

"Wow, we lived on the Market Street side until we moved in this house a couple of years ago."

"That's what's up, shit I'm surprised we never bumped into each other. How long you and Bonz been kicking it?"

"We're not kicking it, that's my older brother," she said laughing showing a white beautiful Colgate smile that had him stuck on stupid.

"Oh shit, my bad," he said laughing.

"Don't force it. It's no big deal, you didn't know. So, you got a girl? And don't be like other guys who front and lie?"

"Well not really, shit ain't poppin'," he said lying not wanting to fuck up his chances of getting with her, and besides his heart wasn't into Lauren. He cared, but not to the point where he was willing to stop fucking with other chicks.

"So maybe we can go out sometime, and chill."

"On some real shit that might not be cool. I mean your brother is my dude, and might not be feeling you fucking with a thug."

"Oh, I get it, you're like everybody else and afraid of him. I'm 19 and I do my own thing. My brother don't run my life."

"Nah, I ain't afraid of him or the next nigga. It's more of a respect thing, you feel me?"

"So you're telling me you're not feeling me like I'm feeling you?" she said looking him straight in his eyes.

"Nah I can't fake the funk. No doubt a nigga likes what he sees I mean what nigga wouldn't want to fuck with you. Your dumb beautiful," Harlem said locking his eyes on hers.

"So, let's get together sometime and have some fun. Shit I'm not asking you to wife me up. I just want to kick it" she said walking over to the couch where he was chillin'.

"Check the move, Asia. If we did fuck with each other it would have to be on the low-low for real, cause I'm not trying to get caught up in no bullshit. I'm not that nigga."

"Why you stressing?"

"I'm not stressing shit. Hit me with your math and I'll hit you up."

They exchanged numbers and she tried to hit up Bonz again, but he didn't answer. Harlem had to meet up with his P.O., so he had to bounce. On the way out the door she pulled him close and kissed his big lips lightly catching him off guard. He couldn't front that shit tasted lovely and he definitely wanted another dose of it. And made a mental note to get back at her with the super quickness. He knew in his heart he should just wave the chick because he knew Bonz would be on some funny shit about the situation. But something inside of him wouldn't allow him to press pause. He felt there was something special about her and wanted to peep what it was. He also knew that Lauren was a major headache when she got a whiff of him moving on other chicks. And didn't want to cause any static with her especially being pregnant. He said fuck it, it was about him being real to himself, and it wasn't that serious. If anything he would just fuck with her on the low and if they do go out and kick it, they would do it far away from Lowell where a million eyes and just as any big mouths were waiting to put shit on the ghetto news. After all to keep it a buck it was Asia that pushed up on him hard body, and what nigga in his right mind would turn down a chick as dope as she was? You would have to be a cold blooded sucker or on some homo shit to turn her down, and Harlem was far from a sucker.

He jumped in the Range, and headed towards the courthouse taking anything out of his pockets that would trip the metal detector, and making sure he wasn't carrying anything he wasn't supposed to be carrying. Last time there he was pulling shit out of his pocket to put into the basket so he could go through the detector and he pulled out a bag of percs that he forgot was in his pockets.

He was dumb lucky the officer was busy answering a question from someone looking for where the Jury Room was located, and didn't peep the move on the package of percs. Harlem stuffed them shits back into his pocket madd quick. He checked himself mentally knowing that shit would of cost him a few years. He made sure there was no more slippin' cause it would fuck with him to the fullest if he got bagged for not staying on point.

The courthouse was packed standing room only. There was news reporters everywhere, he found out all the hype was because they had just arrested this Priest who had molested three boys over a period of four years and used his collar to hide behind. Some even accused the Church of allowing these type of things to occur with immunity. The judge had to bang his gavel a few times to get control of the proceedings. He was heated that his courtroom was not being respected. Because when the Priest's name was called, he stood up in the prisoner's dock to answer to the charges and when the clerk read off the charges, the whole court room went ape, everybody started screaming and yelling at him calling him a fucking nasty ass pedophile and a disgrace to the Catholic Church. They had to separate him from the rest of the prisoners when he went back downstairs to the holding cell awaiting transfer to Billerica jail, because they knew if they didn't there was a chance he would be killed for what he did to those kids.

Shit around the hood had been going well up until a big fight between the Bridge Street Mobsters and the Belvidere 460's at the Black Festival in Shedd Park over a major drug spot being robbed that ended up in the shooting of eight people, with two dying. Rumor was that the Centreville kats got word from the streets that it was the Belvidere 460's that ran up in there and took their shit, tying up everyone in the house and pistol whipping an old lady that stayed there, breaking her face open something ugly and she had to get seventy-six stitches.

Popo began putting madd heat on niggas, raiding spots and posting up on blocks so hard that niggas' custies was madd shook and they couldn't clock money like they were used to clocking. The violence also brought in crazy feds with a license to ill and they went all out pressing any and every one. Shit, they were holding interrogations on the streets, fuck taking niggas downtown.

City Counselor Tran had called an emergency meeting because of the robbery at the drug spot in Centreville where a large amount of drugs and money were taken. They needed to get to the bottom and find out who took the shit and if not, then them BSM niggas will be held responsible for paying for the shit regardless. They're the ones that took it on consignment. One of the rules was the Commission never ever took shorts or loses, and that was just the way it was and niggas knew that when they got down.

Tran also wanted to pull niggas' coats to what he was hearing down at City Hall where he was able to get or intercept all the info that came through there. Lately his colleagues, along with Law Enforcement, have been talking about the City Manager Thompson meeting with the Feds and discussing city problems of priority and requesting the assistance of top law enforcement agencies in helping to take down those who were wreaking havoc on the city streets through violence and drug trafficking and that they were planning on a large scale raid, scooping up all the major players and dismantling the city's drug and gang operations. Word was that someone lips was loose and was hitting the popo with anonymous tips as to what was really going down and who was involved. They received some names including a few high profile people who worked for the city. These names caught the attention of the Feds and Internal Affairs, which meant the stoolie had to be someone inside the circle with intricate knowledge, and the Chief made it known that they needed to find out who it was and put the nigga to sleep before he puts everybody behind prison walls fucking up the whole program and agenda of the commission.

Chief Ryan was on the golf course when his phone rang, he checked it and saw it was from Lt. Cregg one of his partners in crime. They had come up in the ranks together, and their wives hung out, shopped and went to bingo together. He and Cregg had the same attitude and belief about the system since day one and felt that the only way they could live the type of lives that they dreamed of and felt they deserved was to make their own moves, bending the rules and making backroom deals that were highly beneficial to their careers and bank accounts. They felt the people and drug dealers they were trying to lock up were living lavish and stuntin' hard while they were beating the streets and living on bullshit incomes. The lifestyle of a policeman was on bum status compared to the lifestyle these drug kats were living. They turned it over and over in their heads and it never made sense to them. They figured the only way was to move in the ways of the dog eat dog world. He answered the phone.

"Ryan here, what's going on?"

"We gotta talk, it's very important. There's talk and Internal Affairs is snooping through the station asking questions."

"About what?"

"Just questions. The fact that they're here is bothering me. And I, I, don't know Chief. Maybe it's a good idea if we shut it down until things cool down."

"Get a hold of yourself, they're probably here due to the gang violence and murders. Lord knows, it's out of control. There's no reason to worry and we are not aborting the operation, just relax and stay focused."

"But they're all over this station and this city. I'm just cautious I guess."

"Good. Stay cautious. Not a problem. We will be okay. Now let me finish this game. I'm about to beat Senator McKenzie for five grand," he said hanging up.

Chief Ryan had been using Lt. Cregg's associations to clean up the money he was making off of the gangs drug operations. Cregg's brother was affiliated with the Hells Angels, and had a way to launder the money for him through their business ventures. He and Cregg had used some of the proceeds to open up a Gentlemen's Club in Burlington, and buy a hotel on the same property which he put in his sister Jane's name. She was a local real estate attorney who was successful in her own right. So Chief Ryan had no worries about Internal Affairs because they would not find anything that they could get him on unless of course Cregg turned on him, for he was the only person who knew everything. ❏

CHAPTER SEVENTEEN

HARLEM HAD GOTTEN A TEXT that his mom's boyfriend had beaten her up, so he and Lethal went to his crib. After seeing his mom's face he blitzed, and charged into the bedroom and began beefing with the nigga. Lethal moved on dude also, beating him with the butt of a 40 cal. Harlem's mom jumped in and started hitting Harlem and Lethal, yelling for him and Lethal to leave him alone and get out of the house. They ignored her, and kept taxing dude.

"Yo, are you stupid or something? You got this nigga beating you down like a dog, and when I come to check this nigga, and let him know putting his hands on you was a bad mistake, you turn around, and instead of getting your licks in on him, you fucking jump on me? Telling me to leave and kicking me out? When it's this nigga you should be throwing out! What the fuck's wrong with you?!" he asked staring at her angry and confused. "Nigga I don't owe you no explanation! This is my house! Just get your boy, and both of you niggas get to stepping right the fuck out my house! I'm tired of your stupid shit thinking you this and that. Just get your shit, and get out before I call the police and your probation officer."

"Yo my nigga, let's be outta here. The nigga's done up already. Look at his busted up face. And she's tripping something crazy," Lethal said stuffing the pistol back into his waist.

"Man, fuck that crackhead. She ain't none of my mom. Bitch used to leave me at the drug dealer's spot as collateral until she went out tricking and shit. A few times she never came back."

"You lying son of a bitch!" she cursed with the most evilest face pulling the door open.

"You know it's true. As far as I'm concern, you can go kill yourself on the street. It wouldn't matter to me. You were never there for me anyway. Smoking that shit and selling your ass was more important than me." Harlem was so tight that he started hitting the nigga again, and Lethal jumped in again. His mom went and grabbed her celly saying she was calling his P.O.

"Let me get my shit," he said, and went to the stash. He found shit missing, went back in the room, and went ape.

"Where's the rest of my shit! I can't believe you all stole my shit! What you fucking smoking again?"

"None of your fucking business what I'm doing I'm grown. Yeah, I took some of it. Shit, you haven't paid me rent in three months and since you Mr. Baller Shot Caller, making all this money, and buying jewelry and cars, you won't miss the little shit I took," she said adamantly.

"You know what? Fuck you, ma!" and he started hitting the nigga again, and Lethal joined him. His mom went and ran, and got her celly threatening to call the police.

"Yo, let's go she 'bout to call them niggas on us," Lethal said pulling Harlem towards the open door.

"Man, this shit's crazy. My own mom switching up on me for a sucker nigga that puts the fist to her!" he said shaking his head.

"By the way, you still owe me at least a month's rent. So why don't you give me it in crack?" she said blocking the door with her hand out.

"What? I know you are bugging now!" he said trying to push past her.

"Either I get it from you or someone else. And yes, I fucking relapsed. Shit happens you know. That's what Shelton and I were fighting about. He was trying to stop me from getting high, and had threw out my shit when I went to the bathroom."

"Fuck, that nigga ain't suppose to put his hands on you regardless what you do. And no, I'm not giving you shit. Are you crazy? You just stole from me."

"No problem. See ya, and don't be calling me when they put your stupid ass back in jail." she said pulling out a wad of money from her bra. I'ma get mines." she said waving the money.

"You do that," he said walking out the door.

"And don't come back!" she yelled behind him and slammed the door. ❏

CHAPTER EIGHTEEN

HARLEM AND ASIA HAD BEEN KICKING IT, doing their thing for a minute now. So far, they were able to keep it low and away from Lauren and Bonz's ears. She had called him while he was at the studio, and told him she hadn't gotten her period. For some reason he didn't feel bad or bug out about it. Actually he felt some type of way about Asia, and felt a kid with her would be cool. Besides, by the time Bonz found out it was his, it would already be too late. All he could do was step to him about taking care of his child. Harlem left the studio, and went to pick up Asia and her little brother to go to the doctor's to check on her status. Then they'd hit the mall to get little man the new foamposites that Harlem promised him.

After stopping at Expesso's they turned onto Gorham Street heading to 495. At the light by the Superior Court a maroon Camry pulled up beside them, and started shooting. Harlem, hearing the gun blast and window shatter, smashed on the gas pedal, and ran the red light trying to get away. When he got on the highway he saw that the Camry wasn't following him. He exited and pulled into McDonald's to check on Asia and little man. He saw little man was in the bloody back seat slumped over, with half his head missing.

"I'll call an ambulance! You call your brother!" Harlem said fucked up over what he just saw.

"What?" Asia said standing there frightened, and not able to move.

"I said, call your fucking brother! I think I've seen that car before, and know the niggas who did this. It's them fucking Bridge Street niggas!" he said getting super tight.

The paramedics and police showed up. The McDonald's parking lot was packed with police, fire trucks and paramedics, temporarily fucking up business. They pronounced lil man dead, and then took Asia and Harlem to the police station for questioning. Harlem dummied up saying he didn't see who it was or what kind of whip it was. He was just madd busy trying to focus on getting out of harm's way. They didn't believe him, and sent in a special agent to talk with him to try to get some type of info from him that they could go on. The agent knew of Harlem and had him on his radar as a major player in the drug and gang operations in the city. In fact on the agent's board at the central office he had photos of Harlem and his boys taken from surveillance.

They were aware that he was head of the NC5's, and had been looking into his team and their position inside Lowell's underworld. This was an opportunity for him to perhaps gather some intel on him, or do some type of covert evaluation on him. He knew that things in the city were mounting up into a vicious bloody war with the gangs over control of drug operations and leveling old gang beefs. He had received an anonymous tip that told him he would do right to take a long look at Harlem, which they have been, studying him like a research monkey. So, he was already familiar with him to a certain extent. However this was their first face to face meeting.

They had Asia in another room attempting to interrogate her by another officer in regards to her brother's murder. Shit, she was too shaken up and in shock to listen, never mind talk, and had to be sent to the hospital.

Bonz, as well as members of his family, was at the police station looking for answers. The scene in the waiting area was crazy.

"Well, Mr. Valentine my name is Special Agent Blackwell. I'm with the F.B.I." said a tall, thin white man with fire red hair who was in his forties. He was carrying a file, and Sony tape recorder. He took a seat on the opposite side of the table inside the interrogation room at Lowell Police Station.

"Yeh, what up?" Harlem said sitting back in the chair wondering how much of his time will be wasted.

"Man, someone wants you dead," he said smiling.

"How you figure that? Maybe it was a mistaken identity thing. Shit, it happens all the time with the wrong people getting hit up."

The agent laughed. "Listen we don't have to sit here blowing smoke up each other's ass. There's an 11 year old boy sitting inside the fucking morgue, and I want to know why, even though I got a really good idea of why," he said rifling through papers and photos in the file.

"So, if you know why we sitting in here wasting time? Shouldn't you be out there with them trying to find the killers? Shit I don't work for the police, so it ain't my job to find them," Harlem hoped his sarcasm would register in the agent's mind that he was wasting both of their time.

"That's exactly what I'm doing. Trying to find the killers. And I believe you know who they are. If you would be so kind to tell me, I will go and arrest them, and bring them to justice. And we wouldn't have to sit here playing the dumb and dumber game. But if you'd rather sit here and play stupid with me, then maybe you will be the one to be sitting in the morgue with a tag on your big toe one day. Because if they tried to kill you once, and we don't get them, trust me they will try again, and might just get lucky," Agent Blackwell said hoping it would trigger Harlem.

"I ain't worried about that and I don't know nothing. All I know is my friend's lil brother is dead. That's it," Harlem answered annoyed.

"I figured you'd say that. But let me tell you something Mr. Valentine, or could I call you Harlem?"

"Whatever floats your boat."

"First off, I am not your local police officer. I am a Federal Agent whose success rate in closing cases, finding culprits, and locking their asses up is up close to a 90% rate. Which means, the odds of you escaping prosecution and conviction for what I know you're involved in is slim and none. I've been called to Lowell, and put in charge of an investigation that was formulated to destroy the gang and drug activity in this city, and put those responsible behind bars. And with or without your help I intend on doing just that. Now, if you want to lighten the load on yourself, you can do that by cooperating and telling me everything you know about the murders committed by your gang or any other gang. And by giving me the cartel connection and those who are heading the smuggling of large amounts of drugs and guns into the city. And in exchange for that I will classify you as a CI (Confidential Informant) which will not identify you by name, but by a federal number and perhaps get you immunity or a minimum sentence and the Witness Protection Program upon your release.

I'll be frank with you I know exactly who you are, and what set you represent. I also know you're heavily involved with a lot of the drug and gang activity that is disrupting this city.

I also know that you are aligned with others who run organized crime, and like them, think you are going to get away with distributing drugs on a large scale and perhaps murders that you either participated in or ordered. I also know, and let me make this perfectly clear to you, that we are going to bring you down. All of you, the whole bunch from top to bottom is going down. It may not be today or tomorrow or next week, but it's going to happen," he stopped, breaking to take a sip of water.

"Yeah? Whatever. It sounds good. Are you through though?"

"I'll tell you when I'm through! Now do you think the little boy's brother, who we already know is a top rank member of the Asian

Mafia, is going to let you slide for getting him killed?"

"I didn't do jack! And that's his fucking problem not mine!"

"That's not the way he will see it. Trust me when things like this happen, family is always looking for someone to blame, and since we don't have the actual person or persons to satisfy the loved ones thirst for vengeance, guess what? You are on the menu. Now you can play the tough guy role, and that's fine with me, but I'll tell you from experience watch your back because your life is in danger as well as the lives of anyone you love," he said matter of factly.

"Yo, you trippin' a little too extra right now. I ain't worried bout shit."

"Well, here's my card just in case you remember something, or just want to talk, in case the heat gets too hot out there. Oh, and there's also a number on the back where you can call and be anonymous."

"Thanks, but no thanks. I don't get involved with police things. I'm built much better than that," Harlem said harshly rejecting the card.

"Oh, by the way your name came up on our radar. Word is you were involved with the murder on Kinsman Street that snuffed out the life of Joshua Rivera, a.k.a. Chopper. That murder is very special to the agency because the scum had the audacity to hang two infants, only months old, out of the second floor bedroom window, threatening to drop them. And then killed him as he sat next to his baby's mother on the sofa. You know what's funny about that is back in the days, when there were real gangsters, they never ever touched women or children. They were always off limits. To a certain extent it is understandable when someone is killed because they are playing on the same field. But hurting and terrorizing innocent and helpless victims is something beyond comprehension and intolerable. This new generation of gangsters, pranksters, whatever you want to call them, aren't playing by the rules. So guess what? We will not play by the rules either," he said staring in Harlem's face.

"I have no idea about no Kinsman Street or no fucking babies hanging out no windows. That is definitely not how I would get down if I was down. So I don't care two beans who told you I had something to do with it. Obviously you don't believe it or else you would be charging me with it. Nah, I have no clue what you're talking about," Harlem said stretching and yawning, letting the agent know he was boring him with the bullshit.

"Well, I wouldn't say I don't believe. It's more like it's still under investigation, and waiting for more evidence before we arrest those responsible," he replied shaking his head. "Oh, just to let you know, for every one of you that comes in here not wanting to talk, there is 25 who will. You do know what that means don't ya?"

"Nah, not at all. But I suppose you're going to tell me."

"It means that it's only a matter of time before your name falls off the tip of one of the twenty-five's tongues. Now I'm through," he said picking up the file and recorder, and heading toward the door. "Officer Cox will show you out. Have a nice day, Mr. Valentine."

Harlem said nothing he waited for the officer to come to walk him out of the police station. He saw Bonz and the rest of his family sitting in the reception area talking with a few detectives. When they saw each other their eyes met. Bonz stared at him all the way out the door with the most craziest look in his eyes. Harlem wanted to go over and speak to him, but knew it was definitely the wrong time. The Agent was right. This nigga was really thinking Harlem was responsible for his brother getting killed. He must of felt that Harlem had no business putting his brother in a ride, or going anywhere that he might have had smoke with niggas. So no doubt, in Bonz eyes, that nigga did wrong.

He got back around the way, and saw everybody outside standing on the project side of Salem Street. The police were posted up in a line on the other side in front of the substation.

"What the fuck is going on? Why everybody posting?" he asked Kizz.

"Man these idiots just pulled up deep in like 15 cars and just got out and posted there. Niggas ain't saying much, they just posted the fuck up. So everybody from the basketball courts and who was just chillin' in the park came over here in front wondering why the fuck they out here like that," he said talking fast as shit, like a New York nigga.

"Man, shit is crazy. They had me down that station all day trying to get me to flip and turn me into a snitch. Yo, they shot up that car Mingo gave me, and ended up killing Bonz's lil brother."

"What? My nigga, you serious? Ahh shit, here we go. Yo, that's why them Asian niggas been riding through here for like two hours straight before these police niggas showed up. And they had you down their grilling you trying to turn you into a fucking rat ass nigga?"

"Facts, dawg. They had this F.B.I. nigger talking to me out the side of his fucking neck. But on some real shit, nigger know madd shit, but just don't have all the pieces to the puzzle. But from what he do know, it means some nigga close is moving his lips foul. Cause everything he was hitting me with was strictly inside knowledge that only our circle knew."

"For fact?"

"My nigga, they know about the new connect, the drugs, guns and bits and pieces about the murders. To keep it a buck, it's just a matter of time before they come at niggas with them fucking papers. Believe that."

"It's crazy them niggas really got madd knowledge on what's poppin'. Shit, I told niggas not to be out their flossing and fucking throwing bread around like they picked it off of a money tree. But nobody listened. Shit, now all eyes are on us," Kizz said staring at the line of popo in disgust. ❑

PART TWO

CHAPTER NINETEEN

THE STREETS OF LOWELL WERE BLAZING with all the beefing and pushing up on the block the Feds were doing. Niggas were starting to get shook and because of it started making crazy mistakes that brought them alphabet boys closer, running down on niggas and applying all types of pressure on the game. Niggas were wildin' and doing whatever to keep their cash flow up and their pockets fat. What really brought the fire to the streets was the fact that six people were shot in less than ten days in drug sticks gone bad. Whoever was running up in cribs was taking it to another level and tying up and beating the occupants silly, which was not necessary because they got want they came for and even after that got on some ruthless shit and went ham on those that they had robbed.

Harlem had suspected Mingo as the grimy ass nigga that was pulling these capers and got at him about it but Mingo waved him and denied it. But Harlem knew that Mingo and his brother Murder could easily be on some bullshit like that. Them two niggas was always known for doing bugged out, grimy type shit

The gangs from different sides of the city were tripping and on their own shit. Each crew was heated that they wasn't eating like the North Common 5's, who were taking the big bites from the plate, and getting bread off of their custies. They felt Harlem had the plugs ears, and was getting the work, and cutting it before they got the packages. They all started gunning for Harlem and his team, doing random shit like setting up niggas on the block to be robbed.

They would use fly girls from their hood to bait the niggas who always bit on a big butt and a smile. Shit, a jogger who ran the path up on Fort Hill found one of Harlem's boys named Fourfifth butt naked, and duck taped the fuck up, and left for dead. He was barely alive when they got him to Saint Memorial Hospital. He had told Harlem and his team that he recognized the niggas that snatched him up and that it was them Chelmsford Street kids that caught him sleeping while he was chillin' and trying to make a play with this new thotty he had run into in front of the Gaelic Club, who said she had a girl that wanted a ball of flake. The NC5's got on red alert, suited up and went through their hood like fucking gorillas. That started a war on the streets leaving 3 dead and a few niggas needing physical therapy.

Chief Ryan had gotten word that the Feds were knee deep into investigating him. They were all over the station asking questions, and putting taps on his phones. He couldn't figure out how they got ammo on him, after all he thought he insulated himself enough to stay off the radar. His only thought was that it was Tran who was flipping big mouth on him and running his mouth and sharing inside knowledge to someone who was talking, if he wasn't deliberately hitting them off himself.

Either way he knew he had to tighten up his game and his circle and began an exit plan so that he could come clean when they started sniffing through the dirt. The Lowell Police had discovered a dead body full of drugs inside of the back of a hearse that had gotten into an accident in front of Mill City Barbeque & Brew on Gorham Street. After pushing up on the hearse's owner they found out about the plot and how the drugs were being pipelined into the city. The funeral home director quickly gave Tran's name, and they brought him down to the station to interrogate him. Tran played tight lip and denied any knowledge when they first shot at him, but after they found more pieces of the puzzle, they got back at Tran with a full court press who then hit them with some shit, but not everything or enough to take down the Commission.

Harlem's mom went back into detox and left that nigga that thought she was a punching bag, and they had gotten cool again with Harlem moving back in the crib. He never fully moved out, he'd be kicked out one day and told to come back the next, and he was used to it. But after a couple of weeks clean, he had found out through some fiends that had a crack spot on Cabot Street that his mom was back to some grimy shit and getting high hard body and that she had been seen getting in and out of cars on Westford Street and not looking like herself. Harlem knew it was bad because a few times while he was out in front of the house friends of his mom would come by to check on her and to bring her to NA meetings but she was always out saying she was working extra or out with her man.

Truth was she had lost the job at the shelter after being caught smoking crack in the closet during one of her overnight shifts. and had stopped going to meetings. Harlem knew shit in her life was about to get real ugly once again. ❏

CHAPTER TWENTY

BONZ WAS IN THE SHOWER when his celly went off. It was from Clepto, one of the Asian Mafia hitters that came up from California that Bonz was going to use to do the dirty work of the Chief's, who had paid him to get at Harlem and his team for the stash house being robbed. He really didn't have any clue who actually did it, but when they held the meeting to discuss it Harlem showed up with Lethal who was acting really bugged and fucked up making the Chief feel as if he knew about it or had something to do with it. The Chief didn't like black people anyway because he thought they were the ones that killed his dad on Bowers Street, for those who were trafficking humans for prostitution, so it was easy for him to make the decision to go after Harlem and the NC5's off the rip. His plan was to make every crew pay, since no one came forth and he knew one of them did it or had it done, and he was going to make sure each crew knew fucking with him was a no win.

Bonz got out of the shower, checked his messages and saw the text from Clepto that told him they would be ready in about a half hour. He saw his sister on the couch holding her stomach.

"Yo what's good with you?" he said walking towards the entertainment center and plugging in his phone.

"Nothing just sitting here. I just woke up with a ugly feeling like something bad was going to happen."

"Yeah, well that's nothing new. Bad shit happens every day in this crazy mixed up world, look what happened to lil bro. Shit, the whole family has not been the same since he was killed," he said with a tight screw face.

"I know," she said sadly.

"So what's the deal Asia, are you keeping the baby? I mean you got your whole life ahead of you, although in some ways I really want you to keep it. I mean it might help to relieve some of this pain in the family from losing lil man."

"Well, today is the day I gotta make the decision. To be honest I want to, I mean Mom and Dad think to keep it is a bad idea because of me still being in school, but I really want to cuz it's mine, and it's growing in my stomach," she said seriously rubbing her belly.

"Yeah I feel you. That's my nephew in there, and I say have it, and name it after Bravian. And don't worry I'll help you out with him. You will be good, and we will love him to death," he said putting on his Northface to head out.

"Thanks, I think I will, and where are you going this early, I mean why don't you go to the doctors with me?"

"Can't. Shit is about to get real. That nigga Harlem is about to get his just due," he said seriously.

"What, you mean to tell me you're still blaming him for Bravian being killed?"

"Who else is to blame? That nigga knows he was wrong for even having him around his hot ass," he said angrily.

"Brother, he's gone, and you could go kill the whole world and guess what, he'd still be gone. Whether you see it or not Harlem feels almost as bad as we do. He's been over here constantly trying to apologize to you. Mom and Dad have forgiven him, and so did I. Why are you still blaming him?"

"Well, I am about to forgive him in my own way. And you need to stop acting like a public defender. How the fuck you think I look if I let this shit slide? No matter what, lil man got killed in a car he was driving and that's good enough for me. He's fucking guilty, now mind your own business, Asia."

"Mind my own business. Why you buggin' on me? I thought you and Harlem were cool. You know he didn't mean for it to happen, or know it was gonna happen."

"Yeah, we were good, but he took something away from me that was way more cooler than him. Anyways it's not your problem. Trust me I got this. All you gotta do is worry about my nephew. I'll worry about Harlem."

"Well, I can't do exactly that. I mean, maybe you need to sit down brother," she said letting out a small breath of air.

"Yo, I don't have time, I gotta be out. We'll kick it later."

"No. I gotta tell you something I think you should know, before you go on your blitzing mission."

"Yeah, what's that?" he said walking over to cop a squat next to her.

"Well, I lied to you," she said fighting to get the words out.

"Bout what?" he asked giving her an intense look, and rubbing his chin slowly.

"This is not Dimmy's baby," she said looking down at the rug avoiding eye contact.

"What you saying right now, Asia? This ain't no time for jokes," he said standing up over her.

"It's not a joke. It's not his."

"You buggin right now. What the fuck kind of game you playing? And who is the baby daddy?"

"It's Harlem's baby. I told you it was Dimmy's because I was afraid that you, Mom and Dad would get mad if I told you I was having a baby with a black kid. We were always taught to never go out of our race and mix with others, so I lied and said it was Dimmy's. But it's not, it's Harlem's."

"Don't fucking lie to me," he said raising a balled up fist.

"I'm not! Harlem wanted to tell you the day I told him, but I begged him not to because I was afraid I would be forced to have an abortion. This baby, your nephew, is going to need a father," she said rubbing her stomach.

"You know what Asia? Fuck you, how could you trip like that? How can you fuck with a street nigga? What good did you think would come out of that? He's a fucking petty gangster and wanna be rapper, Asia! A fucking ghetto crumb snatcher! He's no good for you," he said pacing back and forth.

"In my eyes you're all the same," she said.

"He's not like me. What type of shit you on, huh?" he screamed.

"Well, he's my baby's daddy, and if you kill him then..."

"Then what?" he said cutting her off.

"I promise you I will kill myself and this baby, and then you can answer to Mom and Dad," she said sincerely with tears falling from her eyes.

"That dirty fucking nigga. I knew them people couldn't be trusted, I knew it. I don't fucking understand how I slept on the sheisty motherfucker. But it's all good. I got something for his ass. Yeah, I got something real lovely for him," he repeated to himself.

Bonz got on his celly and hit up Clepto. "Yo fool, there's a change of plans. We'll still meet up at the spot and go over the new shit. Aiight my nigga?"

"Yo, you good?" Clepto asked detecting some different shit in Bonz's voice.

"Yeah, I'm good," he answered looking at his sister with a smirk on his face.

"Cool, meet you there."

"Alright, one."

"One." ❑

CHAPTER TWENTY-ONE

AGENT BLACKWELL PULLED UP to the beautiful home on top of Andover St. and got out and walked around, giving himself a tour of the gigantic house. There was a gazebo in the back and a huge swimming pool and a pretty decent size pool house. He peeped that there were also a couple of Luxury vehicles parked on the side of the house. He knew there was no way the Chief could afford to live this lavish, unless he was supplementing this the crooked way, and he couldn't understand why no one hadn't taken the Chief down by now. Shit, it was obvious he was on some bullshit, and getting this type of money the dirty way. After finishing soaking everything in he went to the front of the crib and rang the doorbell.

"Who is it?", a woman's voice asked from the other side of the huge wooden door.

Agent Blackwell put his badge up to the security camera that was up in the corner of the door. The door opened slightly and a middle aged woman who was dressed in a designer skirt and blouse greeted him. He couldn't take his eyes off the jewelry she had on. He quickly calculated that it must of costed a small fortune.

"Good afternoon, I'm Agent Blackwell. Mind if I come in and talk to you for a few minutes?" he asked in the most pleasant voice he could muster up.

"Well yeah, but my husband is not home. I'm sure it's him that you want to talk with," she said looking him up and down with curiosity.

"Well no. I mean yes. What I mean is, yes I want to talk to him, but right now I'd be happy to have a quick conversation with you. Is that alright?" he said fumbling to get his notepad out of his pocket.

"I ... I guess so," she said.

"Quite a nice place you guys got here Mrs. Ryan," he said with slight sarcasm.

"Yes it is, I've been told it may be a bit much, but I like it," she said seriously. "Oh pardon my manners, Agent. Would you like something to drink?" she said heading toward the bar in the corner of the room that seemed to be filled with every type of liquor possible.

"No way, and no thank you. Not while on duty. It's hard enough to focus already with this brain of mine. But I would accept a cup of black coffee, no sugar, no cream," he said with a short smile.

"That would be fine. Have a seat, Agent. I'll be right back. I just actually made a pot," she said leaving the room.

Agent Blackwell took off his overcoat, and laid it on the corner of the couch and begin to look around, examining family photos, medals that were on the shelve above the huge fireplace, and the two buck heads up on the wall in between two huge rifles.

"Here you go, Agent. Hope you like it hot, hot," she said smiling, and handing him the cup.

"Indeed I do. Thank you," he said cheerfully and pointing to the medals.

"My husband's. Most of them he got from the Navy, and a few from the Lowell Police Department. The trophies are my late son's. He used to run track for Lowell High, and was pretty good at it. Actually cross country was his favorite," she said proudly.

"That photo seems to be taken in Europe or something," he said pointing at two people standing on top of a mountain with huge smiles on their faces.

"My late son, Jr. and my daughter Meagan. Yes, you're right. It is Europe. How did you guess that?" she asked looking up at him.

"The buildings in the background seem like something out of Ireland. Your late son, huh?" he asked holding the photo close and examining it.

"Yes. Jr was killed in a car accident by a drunk driver on Rt. 110," she said sadly.

"Sorry to hear that, Mrs. Ryan," he said sincerely.

"Thanks. They say time heals all wounds. I don't know about that. I do know a parent is not supposed to bury their child," she said matter of factly.

"How about Meagan?" he asked.

"She's our pride and joy. She's had her share of trouble with usual stuff like drinking and drugs. At one point we thought we was going to lose her also. But she's been clean and sober now for a few months, and attends NA and AA meetings regularly," she said proudly.

"She's a recovering addict? Good for her," he said surprised and looking at a photo of a young lady who he would of have never ever believed was an addict.

"Yup, she's doing good."

"Her drug of choice?" he asked carefully.

"Heroin."

"Well, Ma'am, I don't want to waste your time, but I have to ask you a couple of questions," he said putting the photo down and heading toward the couch.

"Okay, what is this about?"

"Well, I'm just trying to track down the source and suppliers who are pipelining drugs into our community. As you know, this is a deadly epidemic we are dealing with and it's destroying and taking the lives of our kids, and destroying our city," he said looking intently at her trying to read her body language.

"Yes, it's in the Lowell Sun every day that someone is dying of an overdose. But what does my husband or my family have to do with it? I told you, my Meg is clean and off of drugs," she said.

"That's what I'm trying to find out Mrs. Ryan. Your husband's name came up and I'm just routinely checking so that we can eliminate him, that's all," he lied.

"Well, I don't see how I can help you. It's probably best that you ask him."

"Mrs. Ryan, has your husband been acting strange?"

"What do you mean by strange?"

"You know secretive, staying out all night, you know different?"

"No, things have been pretty normal and routine around here with him," she lied.

"Have you or your husband received an inheritance? I mean this is a huge house and you got some top of the line vehicles out there," he said taking another sip of his coffee.

"Well yes, I did get an inheritance. Plus my husband hit the lottery and won close to a million dollars. Why these type of questions, Agent?"

"Oh he did, huh? Well, I guess that explains a lot of things," he said knowing he had already found out about how the Chief came up with the lottery ticket, and probably lied to his wife about it.

The phone rang. "Excuse me," she said going to the table to answer the phone.

"No problem," he said.

"Well, I have to be going. I have a doctor's appointment and my sister is outside waiting."

He got up from the couch and grabbed his jacket. "Thanks for your time, Mrs. Ryan, and the coffee."

"Not a problem, Agent," she said.

"Have a pleasant day," he said extending his hand, and then headed for the door. He then abruptly stopped. "One more question Mrs. Ryan. How much is this house worth?"

"I really have no idea. My husband handled the deal," she said lying. ❑

CHAPTER TWENTY-TWO

MINGO HAD GOTTEN INTO A HUGE BEEF with his girl about her kicking it with her ex. He had peeped it on her Facebook page when she left her phone in his car. They'd been beefing over this situation for a minute now, and each time it would have Mingo extra tight. Last time they got into it was out in front of J's Variety where Mingo's barber was. He heard dude had said some stupid shit about him. When Mingo saw him he approached him, and the nigga got fly out of his mouth. Mingo busted his ass. Mingo and him both got kids by this chick, and she always be playing head games with the niggas getting them caught up in all types of drama. Mingo couldn't believe she had been back to fucking with this nigga. He had always thought she was on some slick shit, but she always talked her way out of it. Since he didn't have any proof he would always let it slide.

This time with proof in hand he went to hunt her ass down, going from nail salon to nail salon like a fucking lion stalking its prey. When he caught up with her at the nail shop next to Jayden's Fresh Cutz he went ill. She denied everything. He knew she was lying, told her to go fuck herself, and threw her phone on the ground and stepped on it. His Timbs demolished the IPhone into pieces. The women in the nail salon was all pushing 911, and with the quickness the popo was there. Mingo was arrested for disorderly conduct, and destruction of property. When he got to the Police Station and was being checked, they peeped he had drugs on him. They found eleven forties of white and nine forties of Brizzy. The bail commissioner set his bail at ten stacks that night. The next morning, he went to Lowell District Court and the Judge lowered it to five stacks.

Harlem and Kizz both showed up in court for the nigga. Mingo's lawyer pushed up on them, and handed them a small kite. It told them the combo to Mingo's safe at his crib, so they could go and get the cash and come snatch him up. If they were able to get it done ASAP, then they could come back to the courthouse, and bail him there before transportation came for niggas. If not, then they would have to go to Billerica House of Correction, and snatch his ass up there.

Harlem had shit to do. Tran and the chief had started acting funny with him, plus Asia had called warning him about Bonz trying to run down on him. He also had to go to a Lamaze class with Lauren, so he didn't have time to make moves for Mingo.

"Yo, Kizz. Go handle that biz for Mingo, and hit me when he's out, my nigga," Harlem said walking towards the Range.

"No doubt. You got that. I'm on it," he said.

"Yo, and tell that fool nigga to leave that no good baby momma of his alone. She keep putting that nigga in the jailhouse. That shit's not cute, my nigga."

"Yeah, he need to. That shit's coldblooded wack, ya heard?" Kizz said shaking his head.

"Facts, aiight my nigga. Get up with you lata."

"Facts."

"One," Harlem said staring at this white shorty getting out from the back of a Chelmsford Police car in handcuffs.

"One hundo, my nigga."

Kizz hit up Mingo's crib on Butterfield Street, and headed to the safe. Checked the paper the lawyer gave him, pushed some numbers, and the safe opened. Inside Kizz peeped DVDs, some weed and some other shit. He looked around and found some fonta leaves. He fell back on the couch, and rolled up, trying to get his head right before going up to the jail to snatch Mingo. Kizz grabbed a few of the DVDs, and fed five into the DVD player. Two minutes into peeping the screen he was stunned. He saw a woman's head bobbing up and down between Mingo's legs. When he saw who it was, he couldn't believe it. It was Mrs. Valentine, Harlem's mother sucking Mingo's dick. He was fucked up. He looked at the blunt of weed, strangely thinking the weed was just that gorilla that it had him seeing things. Then he moved his eyes back to the screen.

"Oh shit! No, he didn't! Oh shit," he repeated.

Mingo was known to trick off with the hoes that were out there. He and his brother Murda always would find some chic down on her luck, and bring her to the spot to get some neck. They was bugged out like that, and even videotaped the shit. Shit, a few years back Murda was fucking with this thotty whose nigga was on lock, and ended up taping her giving him some neck. Then the stupid nigga started showing motherfuckers because the chick refused to do it again. The news traveled to the joint, and when Champ heard it he vowed to see that nigga Murda. When Champ got out he ran down on Murda outside of Captain John's, and beat him with a bat. Murda was in a coma for three weeks, and had crazy staples in his head. But that shit still didn't stop them from doing that shit.

Now Mingo has done the dumbest shit by tricking with Mrs. Valentine. When Harlem found out, he was definitely going to be on some Murder She Wrote type shit. Kizz snatched up the money, ejected the tape and put it in his book bag. He knew he had to tell Harlem, but didn't know if it was the right thing to do. It was definitely going to be some extra shit jumping off. ❑

CHAPTER TWENTY-THREE

CITY COUNCILOR TRAN HAD SEEN THE CAR outside his crib following him. He knew the FBI was closing in, and that soon shit was going to hit the fan. His friend, who owned the funeral parlor who had ratted on him, went into the Witness Protection Program for fear of retaliation. Tran knew that it was only a matter of time before they came back at him and put those silver bracelets on his ass. They said they would be extra easy on him for cooperating if he helped them bag the chief. Since they came at him he hadn't been able to get a wink of sleep. He was afraid that at anytime they would be knocking on his door to lock his ass up, especially when they found out he didn't give them the full scoop. His wife even noticed a fucked up and strange change in him. He hadn't hit her with what was really popping off. Tran was crazy scared that not only was his career in jeopardy, but that he would eventually go to prison for his role in the Commission. He began to get his affairs in order, and wrote a sad and long ass letter to his family explaining everything. When he finished writing, he went out on the back porch to look out over the city and think.

"Honey", his wife of 32 years called, coming up next to him and slowly rubbing his back.

"I was just trying to get some air," he said lying, and continued looking towards the sky.

"Are you ok? You have not been yourself these past few weeks. What's going on?" she said in a concerned tone and voice.

"Nothing. Everything is alright. Just tired, I guess."

"Tired. Is that why there's tears forming in your eyes? Why don't you talk to me?" she asked.

"I'm okay. Really honey. Just a lot on my mind that's all. What time is Lu coming home?" he asked not looking at her.

"She has to work for one of her co-workers. She should be home in a couple of hours. Oh my! I left the rice cooking on the stove!" she said hurrying back into the house.

Tran made a call, and left from the back porch to meet his sister at her restaurant. When he got there, he noticed they were having a little family party. Agent Blackwell had him followed there, and thought it would be a good place to confront him again. He felt by doing it in front of people that Tran knew and loved, he would have a better chance of milking him.

Tran was sitting at the table with a few friends and family when Agent Blackwell sat down next to him, and introduced himself. Tran had already been interrogated by a junior agent, now he was being stepped to by the big dawg: Senior Agent Blackwell.

"Hey, City Councilor, my name is Agent Blackwell. I know you have already been spoken to by someone from our office, and we appreciate your cooperation. However, I believe you left a lot of things out. And if you would be so kind to speak with me, maybe we can resolve this, and at the same time help you out greatly, if you know what I mean?"

"Can we talk somewhere other than here?" Tran said shakily.

"Well, I'd rather not Councilor. I just need to ask you a few questions, and I will be out of your way."

"About what now, Agent? I already told them what I know," Tran said.

"Yes, you did tell us as much as you wanted to tell us, but not everything," Blackwell said staring Tran straight in the eyes.

"Well, I have nothing more to say. I want a lawyer," Tran said nervously.

"Lawyering up, huh? Well, Councilor, you don't have to talk. How about you just listen. We know more than you think we know. We also know that we will get everyone involved. It's just a matter of time. And guess what Councilor? Time is evaporating quickly, and whoever is involved is standing on quicksand.

Let's say you do the right and moral thing. You make a formal statement, and help us dismantle this drug and violence machine that is wreaking havoc on our streets, and killing our kids. In return, we will ask the judge for leniency. This is your last and only shot to come clean, and get your conscious cleared. If not, then let me promise you, when I do get you, and I promise I will, you will be charged to the fullest extent of the law. And you'll find yourself vacationing for the rest of your natural life in a cage about the size of your bathroom with a big ass black man named BB, (Booty Bandit). It's your choice Councilor. But I'll tell you, I am close to solving this puzzle; a lot closer than you think," he said this all the time intently looking at Tran's face and studying his body language.

"I need to think about this," Tran said visibly shaking.

"You do just that Councilor. Here's my card. Call me within 48 hours, or I'll be coming to see you," Agent Blackwell got up, and headed for the door. "Folks, have a good evening," he said tipping his hat at the confused and stunned people sitting around the table. ❑

CHAPTER TWENTY-FOUR

HARLEM WAS AT JAYDEN'S FRESH CUTZ getting his regular taper. He was talking to the usual Saturday crowd of niggas, who was trying to get their shit tight for the show later that night. Shit, Lowell was about to be turnt all the way up, especially with Young M.A and A Boogie about to bless the stage at the Tsongas Arena. Harlem was knee deep in conversation and building with Jay, the nigga that owned the shop, about investing money. They were also talking about their homey, Serious, getting married, and ordained as a Minister, when he peeped the Alphabet Boys roll up in the shop.

"Y'all too late to get a cut. Can't you see how crowded this shop is? And besides I'm thinking no one in here would cut your hair anyways. I mean, when you come through the hood, you're never ever nigga friendly," Harlem said sarcastically.

"Got jokes, huh Valentine? Actually, I came here to check on you. Make sure you were still alive and breathing. I mean, word on the streets is there's a lot of people gunning for you, and betting you won't make it to your next birthday, in case you didn't know that," Agent Blackwell said.

"A nigga like me ain't worried about no shit like dying. What I am worried about is being broke. Real niggas know it comes with the territory. To us living and dying are the same," Harlem said watching niggas' faces break out into smiles, with a couple of niggas saying "Facts," and "You know that's right."

"It's been crazy out in these streets lately. I mean with all the dangerous drugs, gangs fighting, and killing each other, and all the innocent people getting caught in between the ridiculous violence. We were told that if we wanted to cut off the head of the snake that is causing all this madness, that it could be found slithering somewhere on this side of town, so here we are. You don't know where this snake can be found, do you?"

"Like I told you before when you tried to play super cop with me down at the station, I got nothing for you. It's see no evil, speak no evil, and do no evil with me," Harlem said emphatically.

"Not a problem. But do me a huge favor Valentine?" Agent Blackwell said rubbing his chin.

"Yo, you just don't get it. Do it look like a nigga like me would do the Police a favor? Unless the favor would be to make all you motherfuckers disappear, but I'm not David Blaine. You must be really bugging or just can't seem to crack a case," he chuckled.

"Here's my card again in case you lost the first one, next time you look in the mirror tell that snake I'm coming for him., that's if one of your many enemies don't get you first," he said turning around and leaving with his partner right behind him.

"That's a crazy white man right there. His ass be straight buggin'," Harlem said ripping the card up. ❑

CHAPTER TWENTY-FIVE

TOY HAD TAKEN LAUREN TO THE DOCTOR'S for a checkup to see how the baby was doing, and to finally get the ultrasound to see what they were about to have. They left the Doctor's office on Merrimack Str. and headed towards downtown. When they got by the Santander Bank, they noticed this black SUV pull up wildly behind them and a couple of people dressed in all black with masks on their faces rush up to them in broad daylight and in front of everyone just started blazing them up with rapid fire. When they got done they slowly walked back and got in their car, leaving Toy's car looking like Swiss cheese.

It was crazy how they just did it with no type of fear or concern. It was obvious these niggas was used to doing wild shit like that. After all, what bugged out niggas would pull a stunt like that around the corner from the Police Station? When the first responders got there, they found both women slumped hard in their seats unresponsive. In the hand of one of them was a photo of an ultrasound splattered with blood. Lauren was crazy excited and couldn't wait to show Harlem that he was about to be a daddy to a little boy, who she had planned to name after him. But that wasn't about to happen. Because Lauren and the baby had both died instantly, and Toy breathed her last breath right as the ambulance had reached the hospital.

The news traveled fast throughout the city and especially in the Acre. When Harlem got hip to what went down, he became a ticking time bomb, and had vowed to find the niggas who did it, and wipe them and all their families off the face of this earth. His niggas was amped, and were bloodthirsty and put all ears to the street trying to come up with some info on the nutty niggas who fucked with their hood that way.

To add to all the drama, earlier that day Kizz had kept it a buck with Harlem, and told him about what he saw on the tape up at Mingo's crib. Harlem tripped out and went to his mom and told her about the shit and how she was a nasty ass bitch for going out like that, especially with one of his boys and for fucking crack. She denied it and acted like Harlem needed to get some business of his own and stay out of hers. Harlem went into his room and got a copy of the tape he had Kizz make, and threw it on the couch next to her, and walked out the door. His plan was to get at Mingo and break his ass off something proper for violating the bro-code, but after kicking it with Kizz and a few of his other homies, decided to not tell the nigga jack about the tape, and just use the nigga, and treat him like a sucker.

Harlem wasn't crazy positive about who had murked Lauren, Toy and his baby, but he knew it could only be a couple of people that were ruthless enough and would of went after his girl. He knew from Asia that the nigga Bonz had guns for him, and that the Chief also was high on the list, and could have used someone to come after him.

He remembered the last meeting with the Commission, and how the Chief kept throwing innuendos around making him feel like he was blaming the NC5's for the stash house robberies. Plus, the fact that he wasn't invited to the Commission meetings anymore. When he got at them about why they kept waving him and changing from giving him the high-powered drugs to giving him cut up product to sell. They fed him with the bullshit line that it was because he had brought crazy ass Lethal to the meeting and that was an out of the pocket move because everyone knew you didn't bring anyone to their secret cipher. From that moment, the alarm inside of him that lets him know when a nigga is being switched up on went off and it told him that this nigga the Chief was gunning for him and his team.

Chief Ryan was sitting at the Olympia Restaurant eating lunch and reading the Lowell Sun, when Agent Blackwell pulled up a seat and sat down. Chief Ryan just kept reading and ignoring the agent who pulled out his badge and laid it on the table.

"My name is Agent Blackwell. Sorry for interrupting your lunch, but I just got a few important questions to ask you and I'll leave as quietly as I came, that is unless you want to make it easy for me and just confess," he said putting on his glasses and looking at a small notepad.

"Let me ask you something first," Chief said still holding onto the newspaper in a reading position.

"Shoot, go right ahead, feel free."

"Why in the hell did you go filling my wife's head full of your bullshit assumptions?"

"Assumptions, is that what they were?" Agent Blackwell said looking at the chief with a 'come on' look.

"That's all it is, Mr. F.B.I. isn't it? Because you don't have facts, or else you would of already locked me up," the Chief said snickering.

"Locked you up. Well Chief, yes and no. It totally depends on what you say now that will determine if I drag you out of here in cuffs."

"Don't play smart with me. Ask your questions, and stay away from my family."

"And If I don't?"

"This conversation is over," Chief said throwing the paper on the table and getting up.

"Drugs, dead bodies huh? How genius. New house, 3 bank accounts. Sounds like somebody hit the lottery," he said with a slight smile.

"That's exactly what happened," Chief stated matter of factly.

"Or was it City Councilman Green who hit?" he said staring at the Chief.

"I don't have time for this. Come see me when you really have something," Chief said, and began to walk away.

"Oh, I will, and can you do this City a huge and Chiefly favor?" Agent Blackwell said standing up.

"What's that F.B.I Man?" Chief said agitated.

"Stop filling this City with drugs. Can't you see what it's doing?" he said pointing down to the newspaper where it talked about the spike in overdoses. "I mean kids are dying."

"Fuck you," Chief said, and began walking towards the door.

"No, you're the one who's about to be fucked. And oh, what about Meagan? Chief, ever thought the drugs you're flooding this City with, will one day reach her arm?" he said seriously.

Chief Ryan started to say something, but changed his mind and walked right out the door. Agent Blackwell watched him leave, all the while thinking to himself he was going to bring the Chief to his knees. He hated criminals, but hated criminals that were sworn in to protect and serve who went left more. ❏

CHAPTER TWENTY-SIX

CLEPTO AND TREES WERE FOLLOWING Agent Blackwell all the way up Mammoth Rd until they saw him pull into a driveway of a modest green and white house, that had a small plastic pool on the side with a garden hose tilted inside where two kids who looked identical and were about the age of 6 were jumping up and down in it and splashing each other. A pretty woman with red hair was sitting in a lawn chair watching them and talking on the phone. Agent Blackwell walked towards the back of the house where they were. The woman stood up still pressing the phone to her ear and they kissed. He then turned his attention to the two kids who were now splashing and throwing water at him. Clepto absorbed the scene took mental notes and picked up his celly and spoke into it.

"Yo my dude, yeah we found the crib," he said in a whisper type tone.

"Cool, now bounce, we'll see how the Chief wants to handle this. I'll get up with you later."

"Aiight, we out then."

Bonz hangs up the phone and turns to his uncle and the Chief who were in deep conversation.

"Yo, we found the house, now what you want done?", he asked

"Good job," the Chief said. "If F.B.I Man keeps hounding us, put his ass in the ground," Chief said getting up from the table at Dunkin Donuts on Dutton Street.

"No problem, Sir, I'd rather that," he said with a smirk and looking at his uncle who seemed to be crazy nervous.

"For now, just keep tabs and keep the hired guns ready," Chief said.

"They already are, don't you worry I got this," Bonz said putting on his Northface.

"I like this nephew of yours Tran. He has always been a major asset to us," Chief said smiling.

"Yeah, he has," Tran said in a manner that said his mind was preoccupied and somewhere else.

"Well I gotta bounce. Let me know when you want to put him in checkmate. You guys have a nice day," Bonz said laughing. ❏

CHAPTER TWENTY-SEVEN

HARLEM THOUGHT IT WAS THE CHIEF who had Toy and Lauren killed, and that he was also the blame for Kizz getting shot. Kizz had left out of the Lowell Auditorium and was walking to his girl's crib when two niggas ran up on him and started blazing at him. He started running through the College parking lot as bullets flew past him. He almost got away, but he fell and before he could get on his feet again, one of the shooters was close enough to shoot him in the back, paralyzing him from the waist down.

Harlem knew it was the Chief, and had every thought to get at him and even the score up. Harlem grabbed Mingo and they went on a mission to the Chief's crib up on Andover Street. They parlayed in the bushes waiting for him to show up. They sat for hours and when he didn't show up, they snuck into the crib through an open window on the side. They split up to search the house. Mingo found Mrs. Ryan sitting on the sofa putting papers together and stuffing them in a black briefcase, there was also a few large suitcases placed by the couch as if somebody was about to take a trip. He walked quietly behind Mrs. Ryan and put the gun to her head.

"Don't move, bitch. Where is your husband? That's right I'm looking for the Chief", he said and meaning it.

"I don't know," she said lying, knowing damn well she knew where he was.

"Yo lady, I'm going to ask you one more time. Where is he?" He asked again this time in a larger tone and pressing the gun harder to her head.

"Where is the stash, you know money, jewelry and whatever?"

"It's in that black duffle bag over there. Who are you and why are you doing this?", she said pointing.

"Right now, I'm your worst nightmare, and I'm here because your husband is a backstabbing, greedy maggot, and he killed a couple of very close friends of mine, and crippled one of my bros, and now it's payback time! Bitch don't act like you don't know. How you think you can afford a house like this and jewelry like this? In fact, take that shit off," he said pointing to a huge diamond on her left hand.

The Chief's daughter Meagan entered the foyer with a gun aiming straight into the back of Mingo's head. He didn't even know she was there. Out of nowhere, Harlem was standing behind her pointing a gun at her. She didn't peep he was there. Harlem thought about popping her. This was the Chief's only remaining child, and he knew by killing her, it would really fuck the Chief up. Harlem also thought about all that dumb shit Mingo did, tricking with his mom for crack, running around wildin' and bringing crazy heat to the team.

He had not told Mingo about him hearing about it, and since it happened he was waiting for the right time and situation, so he could peel the nigga Mingo's wig.

Instead he put the gun back into the back of his waist, and grabbed up the bag full of money he had found in a ceiling in the cellar. Mingo sat there not knowing, and Harlem, after thinking of all the grimy shit that nigga did, decided to fold on the nigga, and let him be caught up. He backed out quietly. Harlem was about to get into his car, when he heard two gunshots ring out. He knew that Mingo had just got his.

On his way down Andover Street, a Lowell Police car got in the back of him. Harlem knew that if he got bagged with everything in the whip, he was going to be on ice for a long time. He decided to make a run for it and pressed the peddle to the metal, and the cruiser put on its sirens and sped up behind him. Harlem ignored what was behind him, and was weaving in and out of traffic. He got cut off by a pickup truck, and lost control of the vehicle.

He ended up crashing right into the beauty salon on the corner. He was arrested, and got caught for everything in the car. Plus, without him knowing, the day before this happened, he and Mingo both were secretly indicted, and had an arrest warrant for 1st degree murder.

The Judge held him without bail. ❑

CHAPTER TWENTY-EIGHT

AGENT BLACKWELL CONTINUED TO PUSH UP on niggas. He didn't give a fuck. He knew in his heart that all those he thought were involved were involved, and major players at that. He had been assigned to dismantle this drug gang and after five years of investigating this operation, he knew he was about to cut the snake's head off of it and for good. He had the evidence he needed. It came in a manila envelope. It had a long, detailed letter explaining the Commission. It also included a bunch of memory chips from a phone.

A few days prior he began listening to what was on them, and found the crucial evidence that would give him a signed and sealed case. The package was from City Councilor Tran who had committed suicide by blowing his brains out in his office at City Hall. He had written two final letters. One to his family explaining it all from A to Z saying he was sorry for ruining the family name, and that he couldn't nor wouldn't live the rest of his days out rotting in some jail cell. He had fully revealed everything: the guns, drugs and murders, that the Chief was the brains and orchestrator of the death machine that was putting the smash on the City.

Agent Blackwell couldn't wait to put his handcuffs on the Chief, and had planned to snatch him up at his house, but by the time Agent Blackwell got there, no one was there except a black male with dreads lying dead in a pool of blood. ❏

CHAPTER TWENTY-NINE

CHIEF RYAN KNEW THAT TIME WASN'T on his side as far as him walking away from this shit scot-free, especially with all the players and pieces falling apart. A friend of the family who works with the DA'S office had given him an inside scoop on the investigations, and hipped him to the fact that they were about to come hardbody, and snatch his ass up, and the word at the F.B.I. was that they had nearly all the pieces to the puzzle, so that they could destroy the Commission, and lock up Public Officials who were on some bullshit, and would dare to be sitting in City Hall representing the people and at the same time selling drugs to the kids.

Chief Ryan knew they were coming for him, and that the indictments were coming down soon. He had planned for a day or time such as this, and began putting his escape plan into effect. He left that house, job, etc. that morning, telling his wife and daughter they were going on a much-needed vacation. But the truth was they were going away to hide.

The Chief got into his car, and headed to a private little airport in Tewksbury, where he had been learning to fly a Cessna. His pilot was getting the plane ready and gassed up. He had already spoken to his wife and daughter at breakfast, and knew they would meet him there as soon as they finished getting things packed. While he was waiting for his wife he saw about four F.B.I cars headed towards him with their sirens blaring loud. Once they stopped, Agent Blackwell got out of the whip fast.

"Chief Ryan, you are under arrest for running a continuing criminal enterprise," he said with an "I told you so" grin sitting widely on his face.

"Want me to cuff him, Agent Blackwell?" said a tall state-trooper-looking-type nigga who looked like he should be playing on the Boston Celtics, not out here chasing bad guys.

"Nah, I got this one. I'd like to do the honors on this piece of trash," he said pulling out his own cuffs.

"If it isn't big F.B.I man."

"I told you it was only a matter of time. How could you swear to protect and serve the community, and come to find out the City needed protection from you? You're a disgrace to the badge."

He snatched off the Chief's badge and threw it on the ground, and stepped and spit on it.

The Chief's wife and daughter pulled up and got out rapidly.

Agent Blackwell's phone rings. He looks at the caller ID. It's his wife and she put the code so he would know it was an emergency. He answered, "Honey, I am very busy right now. Very busy."

She interrupted him. "They got us at gunpoint, and they are very serious," his wife said clearly shaken up and afraid.

"Who got you?!" he screamed into the phone.

"These two mean guys with masks on. Banged into the house and tied us up. They said when they know the Chief is on the plane and gone, they will release us. The kids are extremely scared."

F.B.I. Agent Blackwell looked at the Chief who had a smile on his face.

"You no good bastard. I should kill you right here, right now!" he said with his face turning tomato red.

"Yeah, yeah, yada, yada. Could you hurry up? I got a vacation to begin," the Chief said holding his cuffed hands up.

"Take the cuffs off that slime ball," he said to the tall NBA looking agent.

"No, no, no. I want you to do the honors. I mean they are your cuffs and keys," the Chief said with a wink.

"I said take them off," he said yelling at his agent who moved toward the Chief.

"No, F.B.I. Man, you put them on, you take them off. I mean we can wait here all day if you want. Just remember your wife and kids are with two of the biggest and ugliest boogeymen they ever saw, with guns pressed to their heads," Chief reminded him.

Agent Blackwell walked over to the Chief and took off the cuffs.

"Now that's more like it. Now where were we?" he said to his wife and daughter, picking up the suitcase and throwing the Nike gym bag full of money over his shoulder.

"You know this ain't over, don't you Chief? I mean you don't think you're gonna just walk in to the sunset do you?" Blackwell said holding the empty cuffs in his hands.

"Put it this way, F.B.I. Man, the day this vacation is over is the day life as you now know will be over. The day you find me is the day you will be burying that pretty little wife of yours. Oh, and those two little crumbsnatchers." Chief said laughing and walking up the stairs of the plane.

"Fuck you, bastard," Agent Blackwell said angrily. "This is not over, Chief."

"You're right, Big Bad F.B.I. Man. Clearly It's just beginning." ❏

* *

A few days after, Harlem was arrested for murder one. He got the news that he was about to sign a nice deal with a major record label. Kane One had put in crazy foot work to try to get Harlem put on because he thought Harlem was nice on the Mic. When he found out Harlem was arrested a couple of days prior, he couldn't believe it. He had gotten in touch with Ms. Valentine asking about Harlem, and wanted to know if he could go see him. He wanted Harlem to know he had made it, and threw it all away.

Ms. Valentine is sober again, and regularly attending church on Grand Street. She dedicated her life to Jesus Christ. She visits Harlem every Friday, and their relationship has gotten much better. ❏

DARRYL E. BUCHANNAN

EPILOGUE – GANGSTA NO MORE

HARLEM SPEAKS OUT FROM BEHIND PRISON WALLS sending a powerful message back to the hood about the crazy cost of playing ghetto games.

Instead of standing on stages all across the world, and rocking the Mic in front of thousands as Hip Hop's newest and biggest star, Lowell rapper Harlem Valentine sits inside of a prison cell about the size of your bathroom. He is now known simply as prisoner #92639. Unfortunately, two days before, he was due to sign and finalize a multi- million dollar recording contract with one the hottest labels in the game. Harlem was arrested by Lowell Police, and charged with two counts of first degree murder.

Being from Lowell myself, and like many I'm a diehard fan of his mix tapes and music which banged hard on social media, and created an out of this world following and buzz that all major labels took notice of, and started one of the most ferocious bidding wars for his talent. Hearing about his arrest took the air out of the rap game for a minute. Harlem's talent and potential was just that serious, and was definitely going to bring him crazy untold wealth and fame. The question on my mind, as I know was on everyone else's mind also, was what would make someone jeopardize and throw his life away? And how did such a success story turn into a tragedy?

I remember the look of unbelief mixed with a smirk on his face as the whole world watched him be found guilty and then sentenced to two life without parole sentences. I swear as I walked around that day, Mill City had a black cloud hovering over it. It was like the hope of the city had gotten locked up with him.

I reached out to Harlem through his mom, got his info, and shot him a kite letting him know I wanted to holla at him, and chop it up with him on a one on one. Not only to give him the opportunity to hit us, his community and fans with the missing pieces to the puzzle of how or what the hell was he thinking, but maybe there was some real shit he could drop on the homies out there in the hood, standing on blocks with a pocketful of dreams and talent in a world of no hope, who are being lured away and enticed by the magnetic pull of the streets, and the knowledge that breeds a self-destructive 'fuck the world' mindset.

A few weeks after flying my kite, I received a phone call asking if I would accept a collect call from a prison, blah, blah, blah. It was Harlem. We chopped it up for a few. He said it was peace if I pulled show at the prison to sit down and build about his situation, the jailhouse politics, and all the B.S. going down in the streets. He said as a real nigga he felt it was his duty to hit the streets with the real facts about being locked up, and playing the ghetto games that were designed to destroy and bring pain in large amounts to a nigga's life. What stood with me long after we hung up the jack was when he said niggas are playing themselves, robbing, stealing and killing each other for a game that is not even real, and that what we call a lifestyle, in reality is nothing but a death style.

This interview took place at M.C.I. Walpole State Prison, a white walled fortress which holds some of the state's most notorious prisoners. In fact, most of the prisoners there are doing sentences that sound like telephone numbers. The fact is many of these behind these walls are gonna breathe their last breath there, and the sad thing is, many of them are young people just like you. Never ever to see the free world again, all because they wanted to be down, and chill with the so called 'tough guys', toting guns, beefing and warring with each other, never ever thinking one day their life would be cut short by a gun or a court system. After all, the game teaches us that we are too cool to get caught or that it's no big deal to be in front of the judge on a murder charge. Unfortunately, the reality doesn't hit someone until they are sentenced to die behind prison walls, many spending thirty, forty, fifty years inside the cages, waiting to die. That's the only way they will ever leave from behind the wall. Trust me, the graveyard and prisons are full with young people who thought it was cool to be gangsta. But at the end of the day, they found out that they were messing with a game they just couldn't win.

At the end of the day someone has to tell you the truth, not the half-truth, not the watered-down version, but the truth, plain and simple. And who better to drop it on you than someone like Harlem who got caught up in the gangsta thug lifestyle, believing the hype on the streets and ended up catching a double life sentence , yo. I really hope you pay attention to what this brother has to say. Shit is real, and it's definitely not pretty to exchange your name for a number.

D.B. Hey Harlem, how you doing, bruh?

H. Man, just trying to make the best of a bad situation. Each day is a struggle in here just tryin' to keep my mental right and tight.

D.B. I feel you. Yo, thanks for sitting down with a brother, and doing this interview. Maybe you can pass a message to a lil homey who may be following down the same path.

H. No doubt. I hope so, because it's ugly in here. I mean niggas out there don't have a clue of what's waiting for them on this side. Man O.G., this shit is all the way too real.

D.B. That's a double fact. Shit I know. I got crazy years behind these walls. It's crazy cause out on the block through videos, music, and other media outlets, prison and doing time is made to look cool, gangsta and a way to get your stripes. The bad thing is a lot us get caught up believing the hype, only to end up here and finding out you straight played yourself.

H. For real. I know for me around my way, getting locked up was looked at like no big deal. It was just another part of the game. You know a nigga out there hustling, beefing, wildin' out or whatever, when you get bagged, you come inside, eat big and get your weight up. Besides you should be good. You think your homey will hold you down with loot for canteen, for your phone, and come through for visits. But yo, that shit is not real. I found out the hard way that all that street talk about niggas riding or dying with you is B.S. cause once you locked up inside of these cages, behind these walls, it's outta sight, outta mind. Nobody rocks with you. You feel like you're on a tiny ass island by yourself waiting to die.

D.B. That's real talk. Everybody forgets you once you locked up. You're lucky if you got one person riding with you once these metal doors slam on you.

H. Yeah, no doubt. You definitely get to peep who's real and who's fake. It's a crazy painful thing when the truth hits you, and you see the reality of things on the flip side. When you're out there busting guns and repping your hood or set, everybody act like it's all love all fam. But as soon as you get in this situation, niggas scatter away from you like roaches. It's bananas, O.G. I can't believe I went out like a cold-blooded sucker.

D.B. Yeah, love grows cold madd fast when a nigga up in here. It's like you just fade to black on people's minds. So, what is a day like for you up in here, bruh?

H. Same shit every day. I just try to stay to myself, do my own thing. A lot of niggas sitting in here with die in jail type sentences, and instead of being in the Law Library, and fighting their cases, they be in the gym playing basketball, or in the weight room trying to get big. Shit, no matter how big they get, they can never carry a life sentence. As for me, O.G., I be in the Law Library every chance I get. I wake up with beefing with these courts on my mind. I get up, get some breakfast in me, pray, and as soon as these doors pop, I'm in the Law Library. And I stay there until they tell us we gotta bounce back to the block for count. After count and chow, I shoot straight back to the Law Library, except on Fridays, when my moms comes through to visit me. I try to stay away from all the negative jailhouse politics and B.S. My days are the same, and if I don't flip my case, this is how I'll be living for the rest of my life. And I'm only twenty-one.

D.B. How old were you when you first joined a gang? I mean there's lil homies out there who think that's what's up. And they are running around the community/city blasting guns and terrorizing everybody. They think that's some cool type of thing.

H. Yo O.G., I wouldn't wish prison on my enemy. Those out there buck wildin' don't know about this side. All the stress, the anxiety that comes with this. Because I didn't know, until I was here and it was too late.

I was eight years old when I first got into gangbanging and wanting to be down. I got caught up in the ghetto games just like all the niggas I grew up with. Selling drugs and gang life was presented as the only way to live and to survive in the environment I lived in.

D.B. What attracted to you to a gang, to that lifestyle?

H. I mean it was what we did. Everyone seemed to be in one gang or another. You had to rep something. I remember being out there seeing dudes driving nice cars, dressing fresh, and having pretty girls around them all the time, and that's what I wanted. When you're a shorty, you can only see the glamorous side, the shine. You don't see the ugliness, and if you do, you're convinced it won't be you. Plus, you see niggas coming home after doing a bid. You don't see them niggas looking sad, like they just left a fucked-up situation. In fact, you see these niggas looking healthy, with big smiles on their faces as if they just went through something light.

D.B. How did you get down?

H. I use to watch the older kids doing their thing. One day one of the homies gave me a backpack, and told me to hold it. So, I did. I brought it in my house, and when they came to get it, I gave it to them. A couple of days later, they gave me a pair of Jordans. And since then I've been down. Shit, money is so tight, plus whatever money my mom was getting, she spent on crack, not on me. So up until then, I never had Jordans or shit like that.

D.B. Was your mom and pop in your life?

H. Nah, not really. My pops has been locked up most of my life. In fact, the first time I ever met him is when my moms brought me to visit him in Walpole. He's locked up in Shirley Max now. My mom was a crack addict most of my life. She didn't stop using until after my trial. Shit, in my hood a father is seldom seen. All we had was each other. Lil niggas raising lil niggas. It's crazy.

D.B. So, you moms is good?

H. Yeah, she cool. She's in church now and comes to check me every Friday. It's been hard on her. When they found me guilty, she fainted, and I straight bugged out in the courtroom. A lot of my boys showed up for trial, but after that, I haven't heard from anyone except Serious. My girl, Asia, bounced with my child before my trial was even over. Imagine that. She didn't even wait to see if I would be found guilty.

D.B. So, Serious comes through, huh?

H. Yeah, no doubt. He pulls show, and keeps a few dollars on my books and the phone. He a pastor now. He the realest nigga I know. It's crazy. This shit wasn't suppose to be like this. I lost my best friend, ColdWorld, my girl, and baby to this shit. And all the other niggas either locked up or dead or out there on drugs. It's crazy. And this way of life is being passed down to the the lil homies. This shit gotta stop.

D.B. You got homies in here? Do you still rep your set?

H. Nah, I couldn't. Not knowing what I know now about how fake the shit is. I mean when I got here I was still on my NC5 shit. But then I saw that niggas in here from all sets are breaking bread with the same niggas they warring with and killing out there on the bricks. Man, that lifestyle ain't even real in here.

D.B. Yo, it's like that for real?

H. Just like that. Real talk. And if you out there doing gangsta shit, remember they got some gangsta-ass time waiting for you. Ain't nothing pretty about this. We fucked up in here, and any nigga that think this shit is cool, is a damn fool. The game is for suckers, straight up.

D.B. Yo, was you ever locked up in juvie?

H. Yeah, facts. I was for possession of a firearm. I was twelve then. They sent me to Roslindale lock-up. Being locked up in juvie wasn't a major thing. They don't teach you nothing, especially how to stay out of jail or trouble. If anything, you learn more crazy stuff, more ways to get into trouble, and you meet badder kids than you. Most of the time we were in there beefing with each other because we repped different sets. You get more game, more connections and become more ruthless. To keep it a hundred, it made me more heartless. Since I've been in, I ran into a lot of kids here I was in juvie with.

D.B. I know you can't talk much about your case, but what did they say you did?

H. They accused me of two murders, and found me guilty of both. One that happened on Kinsman Street, and some other shit out in Haverhill, where one of my boys met a girl off the Book (Facebook). They invited us to a party out there, so a few of us went through to chill and meet up with chicks. Niggas got on some hating shit. A beef broke out, and two of my niggas got shot: One in the arm, one the butt. Three days later they claim a car pulled up on their block, and started spraying. Four people got shot, one died. The police said they were told I was the one that did it. They came to my mom's crib and arrested me.

But like I said I'm fighting my case. That's why every day I be up in the Law Library. Look around, O.G. It's basically empty. It's almost 400 niggas in this prison, and only ten of us in here. And that's how it is every day on a regular. These dudes rather play ball than work on getting free. Not me. I stay in the ring fighting with the Commonwealth.

D.B. I feel you. I would too. What do you think your chances are of getting a new trial and going home?

H. Man, these courts ain't playing. They are straight locking niggas up, and throwing away the keys. I mean I try to stay hopeful and positive. They say every case has a loophole. I'm trying to find it. It may be a needle in the haystack, but if I don't find it, then I will die here. Nah, this shit ain't no joke, bro.

D.B. I got a chance to holla at rep for the record label that signed you. They are disappointed. Said you was going to put the game in a chokehold.

H. Man, I'm so sick to my stomach about that. All my life all I ever wanted was to be a rapper. Rep Mill City, and I believed and chased it. Thought that I could sell a little drugs to buy studio time. And this set NC5 wasn't supposed to be on no crazy B.S. We was just trying to get money, hustle together, and win together. I remember my mom sending me the Lowell Sun article about me. It said, "The newly crowned king of hip hop with a multi-million-dollar contract, threw it all away, and exchanged his name for a number: another case of wasted talent."

To sit here knowing I had it all - the house, the cars, and I got it the legal way, and lost behind getting caught up in the street. It is a hard and bitter pill to swallow.

Can we change the subject? I can't even talk about that. It's way too painful. Way too deep.

At that, tears fell from Harlem's eyes. He wiped them and smiled. Then said, "Nah, it's not a game this life we live."

D.B. Hey, bruh, is there anything else you want to say to the homies out there?

H. Yeah, stay in school, stay out of gangs, and use your head to get what you want. Don't let no one play you into thinking you can't win the right way, and with the mind you got. It might take some time and hard work, but it's better than being behind prison walls every day wishing you were out there. If I could do it all again, I wouldn't get involved with none of the stuff I did. It kills me a little more each day, waking up in this cage knowing I threw my life away for something that was fake.

D.B. Thanks again, bro, and God Bless.

H. Nah, thank you. To the Hood: I hope you heard me!

D.B. Well, there you have it: the truth from behind the walls, from a homey who is living proof of what can happen to you if you get involved with street games. Don't believe the hype that's out there, or you hear or see on TV, videos, and music. The problem is rappers and actors are paid millions of dollars to promote this lifestyle. It's all entertainment to them. They act the part out or rap the part out, and then bounce to their million dollar cribs in their hundred thousand dollar cars. While the lil homey on the block act the part out, and end up in the back of police cars and inside jail cells, if they're lucky. Or in one of those long, black, last-ride limos if they are not.

You got a choice, my homey.

Make the right one.

Author of *A Thousand Thugs*
Darryl Buchannan

A THOUSAND THUGS

PRISONERS EDUCATIONAL COMPONENT
By Darryl Buchannan
Author of *A Thousand Thugs* – September 2017

THIS COMPONENT WAS CREATED TO BE UTILIZED BY PRISONERS to assist them in re-examining their choices and decisions that led to their incarceration. Many behind the walls do not hold the view that their own actions and behaviors placed them in their circumstance. In order for them to benefit and find any solution that will liberate them to provide for a more positive and constructive foundation upon release, they must reach the understanding of the events that led to their incarceration. They must take full responsibility for not only what got them there, but what will keep them from returning once they are released. This component is designed to ignite that process, and allow the participants an opportunity to take a deep look at themselves.

For almost twenty-eight years I was caught up in the lifestyle of going in and out of prison. In the environment in which I grew up prison was viewed as a rite of passage or a way to get stripes. At a young age I was introduced to drugs, gangs, crime and the 'gangsta/thug' mentality, and embraced it wholeheartedly. Reppin' this lifestyle was costly. Not only did I spend too much of my life behind bars, locked inside of a cage about the size of a bathroom, but I lost many of my friends to the streets either through gang wars or drug overdoses and addiction, with myself acquiring a very terrible and lengthy criminal record, and becoming homeless and living the lifestyle of a drug addict. My story is unfortunately the story of many as you can see through the eyes and lives of Harlem and his friends. The characters inside this story reflect the lives of those that can be found on any city street in America, but more so in the youth population.

I hope that Harlem and his friends' story connects with you in a way that will stimulate and motivate change. But more than anything, I hope it answers some of your questions, helps you find solutions, and assists you in breaking the mental, emotional and psychological chains that keep you confined within. If you are sitting in a prison cell asking yourself "Why did I do this to myself?" or "I never want to come here again," then this component was created for you. I hope that you discover what I have discovered. It was MY choices and decisions that led me to prison, to being homeless and addicted to crack ... ❑

Week One: PRISON

PARTICIPANTS QUESTIONNAIRE

1) Now that you find yourself locked up what are your thoughts about it?

2) A lot of people think it's no big deal to be in prison. In fact they accept it as a part of the game or lifestyle. Did you ever see or realize that one day your behavior would put you in jail or prison? Why/Why Not?

3) Everyone fronts or acts tough like being in jail is cool, when in reality I know for me it sucked, especially being told when to eat, shit and go to sleep. The real shit about being locked up is never told. You know the loneliness, frustration, and boredom, not to mention feeling like the world is passing you by. Look at your surroundings. Take a few minutes to really think about your situation. Now tell me on some real shit, what do you really feel about being locked up?

4) Now that you're sitting in prison what things do think you could have done differently that would have helped you avoid the misery of jail?

5) Many of us go to prison, and instead of looking at the real problem and doing something positive that will help us, we instead attempt to avoid the reality and fill our days playing basketball, cards and getting down with the jailhouse politics and bullshit. The problem is just because we avoid the problems that led us to jail does not make them go away. What are some of the things you know you need to work on to change so that you can get out and stay out?

6) In the story Harlem's boy Serious had gotten locked up for gang violence and a shooting in his hood. While there, he made decisions to never go back to prison again. He dropped his set, and began working on bettering himself. He developed a plan on starting his own business, and got out and did the right thing. What plans can you make to help you better yourself? Have you made a list of positive things you like to do? If not take the time to do that, for there is nothing like investing in yourself and your life. ❏

Week Two: DRUGS

PARTICIPANTS QUESTIONNAIRE

1) About 85% of those incarcerated are there because of drugs in some form or fashion. Whether using or selling them. If you take a serious and honest look at yourself, can you identify what and how much drugs played a part in you being locked up?

2) I know for me every time I was arrested for committing a crime, it was a direct result of using or trying to use. I never went to jail unless I was high or trying to get high. In the story drugs played a major role in the destructiveness in the lives of the characters. How about you? Is drugs a main reason you are locked up? If so, explain.

3) In what ways do you see drugs effecting your life, family and the community?

4) While I was locked up I participated in programs not to get real help, but just for the good time or time out of my cell, and in the end I found out I played myself. What are your thoughts about getting help while you're there?

5) Grab a piece of paper and write down the "pros and cons" of using or selling drugs. Try to put every thought down so that you can get a clear picture.

6) Imagine if you didn't use or sell drugs what would your life look like now. Write down all you've lost and another list of all you've gained. ❏

Week Three: SELF-WORTH

PARTICIPANTS QUESTIONNAIRE

1) I remember running the street and feeling like my life wasn't important, or as if I didn't deserve a better life. I mean everything around me confirmed that I was a no good crack addict and criminal junkie, so in some sense it seemed like I had given up. I stopped trying to be somebody or something worthwhile. What are your thoughts about yourself? Why do you feel that way?

2) It seemed like wilding out and using drugs was the answer for the way I was feeling for a long time. Then things turned ugly. I became caught up in a crazy cycle as if I was on a death or suicide mission. I just didn't care whether I lived or died. Have you ever had these feelings or thoughts? Why or why not? Please explain.

3) I remember sitting in prison. Everybody who I thought would be there for me had turned their backs on me. My so-called friends never wrote to me or sent money for my commissary. I remember feeling like a piece of shit, which made me even more angry than I already was, and I hated myself. Have you ever experienced these dreadful

feelings? Why or why not? Can you explain your answers thoroughly?

4) In your opinion what do you think is a good reason for you to change? Please explain. ❏

Week Four: TRUTH VS. LIES

PARTICIPANTS QUESTIONNAIRE

1) In "A Thousand Thugs" Harlem and his boys were exposed to a lot of misinformation about life. It seemed like their whole environment was full of negativity. What types of misinformation were you exposed to?

2) It's so easy to get caught up in the hype on the street. What are some of the lies that you were told and believed about gangs, drugs, and prison? Why did you believe these things?

3) They say the good life is about sex, drugs, and rock 'n roll. What are your thoughts about how important these things are?

4) The main character in the story, Harlem, said that he couldn't believe he threw his life away for a lie. Do you feel you're in jail right not for living a lie? Please explain. ❏

GOALS

Please take a few moments to think about your life and then make a list of your goals.

_____

_____

_____

_____

_____

_____

_____

_____

_____

_____

_____

_____

_____

_____

_____

_____

PLANS

No one really wants to be in jails, sitting inside of a cage the size of a bathroom; a very small space that you have to share with another person. It's time you sit down and put a plan together to insure yourself a better and more productive future. They say if you fail to plan then you plan on failing.

NOTES FOR MOMENTS OF REFLECTION

DARRYL E. BUCHANNAN

NOTES FOR MOMENTS OF REFLECTION